OF DUKES AND FORBIDDEN WORDS

Dashing Rogues and Ruined Librarians
Book 1

Sandra Sookoo

ARE YOU SIGNED UP FOR DRAGONBLADE'S BLOG?

You'll get the latest news and information on exclusive giveaways, exclusive excerpts, coming releases, sales, free books, cover reveals and more.

Check out our complete list of authors, too!

No spam, no junk. That's a promise!

Sign Up Here

www.dragonbladepublishing.com

Dearest Reader;

Thank you for your support of a small press. At Dragonblade Publishing, we strive to bring you the highest quality Historical Romance from some of the best authors in the business. Without your support, there is no 'us', so we sincerely hope you adore these stories and find some new favorite authors along the way.

Happy Reading!

CEO, Dragonblade Publishing

Additional Dragonblade books by Author Sandra Sookoo

Dashing Rogues and Ruined Librarians Series
Of Dukes and Forbidden Words (Book 1)

The Boxers of Brook Street Series
With Love in Their Corner (Book 1)
Go Down Swinging for Love (Book 2)
On the Ropes of Scandal (Book 3)

The Hasting Sisters Series
The Devil's Game (Book 1)
A Second Summertime Courtship (Book 2)
An Impossible Match (Book 3)

Willful Winterbournes Series
Romancing Miss Quill (Book 1)
Pursuing Mr. Mattingly (Book 2)
Courting Lady Yeardly (Book 3)
Guarding the Widow Pellingham (Book 4)
Bedeviling Major Kenton (Book 5)
Charming Miss Standish (Book 6)
Teasing Miss Atherby (Novella)

The Storme Brother Series
The Soul of a Storme (Book 1)
The Heart of a Storme (Book 2)
The Look of a Storme (Book 3)
The Sting of a Storme (Book 4)
The Touch of a Storme (Book 5)
The Fury of a Storme (Book 6)
Much Ado About a Storme (Novella)
A Storme's First Noelle (Novella)

A Storme's Christmas Legacy (Novella)

The Lyon's Den Series
The Lyon's Puzzle
The Lyon's Redemption
Dreaming of a Lyon
The Blind Lyon

Dedication

For Kelly Price. You are such a lovely friend and supporter of my books. Thank you for your insight into my duke. I hope you enjoy him as much as I did while writing him.

CHAPTER ONE

December 16, 1816
Combes House
Grosvenor Square, Mayfair
London

BARRINGTON COMBES-MEAD—THE 10TH Duke of Scarborough—stood at the window of his dressing room clad in navy breeches and a line lawn shirt with his curled hands resting on the cool glass as he stared out at the Mayfair street below.

As well as the incessant rain that fell onto everything.

"You know, Travers, today I turned eight and forty," he said in a noncommittal tone, not taking his gaze from the scene outside. "And do you think the weather could cooperate? Do you think anyone around me would care to drop by and encourage me to celebrate?" He blew out a breath. "No, on both counts."

From somewhere behind him, his valet chuckled. "That doesn't mean you shouldn't do something to mark the occasion, Your Grace. There is much to fill the time with, but I'm afraid that even you can do nothing about the rain."

"There is that." With a sigh, he continued to peer out the window. Despite the horrid weather, a few closed carriages ambled along the streets, the lanterns on the outsides providing cheerful, golden illumination in the gloom. "The damned Christmastide season will be upon us soon as well."

"I am aware of that, Your Grace." The valet came behind him

and fit a waistcoat of gray satin to Barr's torso then did up the laces in the back.

"Yes, well, with everyone scattered, I had hoped to forget this year." He frowned, and watched the reflection of the gesture in the glass. "I had thought life would have been... more than it is by the time the children were grown."

In his life, he'd been blessed with two children, who had both reached their majority. His son was six and twenty, and he'd married last Christmastide. His daughter was two and twenty, but she was quite selective about finding a match and preferred to remain unattached until she could decide what—and who—she wanted from life. The girl had enjoyed three Seasons already to the same results, and that suited Barr just fine. Marriage was forever; she needed to be certain, and he wouldn't force the issue like so many of his contemporaries with daughters.

"Forgetting what has made you essentially... you, is never a good idea." Travers softly cleared his throat. "Could we please complete your toilette, Your Grace? Tea will be served soon, and despite the fact that you are alone, you always enjoy the respite."

"Very well." Barr nodded as he turned about and then padded closer to the open wardrobe where Travers stood, holding out a jacket of sapphire superfine. "Where most people despise the rain, I have never hated it, especially in London, but the recent weather has taxed even my acceptance and patience." He shoved a hand through his hair. "Good God, will it *ever* stop raining?"

"At this time, it is the way of things, Your Grace." The calming tone of his valet's voice was something he needed and appreciated as he held up the jacket for Barr to slide his arms into the sleeves.

"Bah."

They were well into what historians and journalists alike were calling "The Year Without a Summer," all due to a volcanic eruption on a tiny island near Indonesia that no one had heard of, let alone knew had existed at all. Hell, most people in England couldn't pronounce Indonesia, and he suspected half of those people didn't even think of a larger world that went past the bounds of their own country.

National dimness was what happened when education fell only to the upper classes, and no one put any sort of value on the ability to read or write. But then, that was how the men in charge liked things; a stupid population was one more easily controlled, and it kept their fat arses in power.

Bah. A pox on the Regent.

Dismal thoughts indeed—perhaps even treasonous in some circles—made even more so by the daily drenching rains and cold temperatures. Despite the fact that it was December.

Add to that was the fact that the Christmastide season would soon come upon them all, and that would probably prove dismal as well, since supplies coming into the ports were slow and, in less quantities, because crops all around the world had failed, livestock died, and textiles unable to arrive on time.

From one tiny volcano on a tucked-away island halfway around the world.

A humbug indeed.

"You need something to fill your days, something to occupy your time so you can perhaps see things with a new perspective," Travers said as he brushed a piece of stray lint from a corner of the jacket.

Barr grunted in return.

One saving grace of the whole debacle was that England was in a better position than other countries, say America, in that they *did* have many ports and were able to import supplies more often now than in the summer, but things still hadn't returned to good, and no one could predict when that would happen.

Or when the damned sun would ever shine again.

"It doesn't matter how many times you come the crab, Your Grace, nothing will change unless you take that first step."

"Do shut up, Travers. This isn't one of those days when I want cheered up."

All that rain made travel hazardous. He would pass the holidays in London instead of traveling to his country estate, which was near Cornwall, almost in the wilds. Ordinarily, that would suit his soul, for life was very different these days, especially since he'd lost his wife.

An unexcepted ache squeezed around his heart. It didn't happen much these days, but grief wasn't exactly a straight line. It had been five years ago. Some days he was perfectly able to conduct his life, then others, grief held him in a tight grip. Where he'd assumed he'd have a lifetime with Georgiana, fate had other plans.

And had left him very much alone. Which brought his thoughts back to the steady rain drumming on the windows. His two children weren't in London just now and couldn't get back even if they'd wanted to due to the wretched state of rural roads, so Edwin would remain at Scarborough Hall while Beatrice would stay with her cousins—his sister's offspring—in Derbyshire.

Perhaps that was best, for they would each have a lovely holiday season, while it would probably prove more miserable than not here.

Amusement danced in his valet's eyes. His blond hair gleamed like gold in the candlelight. "You can't close yourself off during the Christmastide season."

"I'm not. I'll keep myself busy by finishing the ongoing renovation of this townhouse."

"Which has been lingering since the autumn of last year," Travers said with a raised eyebrow.

"Because of the damned volcano in a far-flung section of the world."

Travers shrugged. "Does it matter? For whatever reason, you are dragging your feet on the renovations. I can only wonder why."

"You know why. So do I." He met the valet's eyes. "Once it's finally finished, I won't have any other projects to fill my time, and I might feel compelled to circulate in society."

"And we both know you will only do that as a last resort."

"Indeed." Barr shrugged. "Come. We're headed for the attics. I want to poke about and see if there is anything up there I can incorporate into the new décor for the drawing room." It had been the room he'd recently finished, and yet now it lacked a certain… something to reflect his personality and the sense of adventure he'd once had.

"Must I?"

"You must. Since you are so keen on giving me advice, you might as well assist me in dragging down a few things." With what felt like a cheeky grin, Barr led the way out of the room. "Shouldn't take that long."

Since no one could travel much due to the wretched weather, Travers consented to spend Christmas in London. That suited Barr just fine because they'd been friends for years, and he was one of the handful of people on the earth that he trusted.

They had been friends since meeting in India where Travers had worked for an English general. When that man retired, since Barr was returning home from checking on his investments with the East India Company, he'd hired him, and they'd been together ever since. The valet had helped him through the grieving process when Barr's wife died five years ago, had been there when Barr's son had married then left for Cornwall.

Conversely, Barr was there when Travers' daughter died of consumption a few years back. The valet's wife served as the cook at the London townhouse, and there'd been many nights, especially in the winters, that they gathered in the kitchen around the hearth, drinking toddies together and playing cards. There was no need to stand on ceremony or demand class divides amidst friends.

By the time the men poked through trunks and boxes stored in the attic section of the townhouse, they were cracking jokes and reminiscing about the antics of guests and children during prior years when he and his wife had hosted Christmastide balls.

"Might I speak freely, Your Grace?"

He glanced at Travers with a frown. "Of course. You know this."

"Thank you." The valet nodded as he sifted through clothing and slippers inside one of the trunks. "In my honest opinion, you do need to put yourself out into society more often. Accept some of the invitations being sent to you, especially during this time of year."

"Thank you for the concern, but I'm not ready for any of that."

Compassion reflected in Travers' hazel eyes. "It's been five years since Her Grace died, Barr. I rather doubt she would have wanted you to ignore everything and hide."

"I'm not hiding." Damn but time passed quickly yet alternately it went too slowly. "Besides, I'm a father."

"Yes, with grown children who now have lives of their own." The valet shook his head and shot him a knowing glance. "That doesn't mean you're dead."

"Perhaps." He set a box away from him that contained nothing more than old miniature portraits of various members of his family, now long gone from this mortal coil. "But I *am* busy with the renovation."

Travers snorted. "Only because you refuse to hire the required number of laborers. It could have been completed months ago."

"True, but I enjoy working with my hands."

"You need to use those hands on a woman." One of the valet's blond eyebrows rose. "In fact, you would *thoroughly* benefit from having a woman in your bed."

Dear God. Was this Travers' new way to badger him, then? "Perhaps, but everyone is disgruntled because of this wretched weather, this even more wretched year. It's best to wait."

"That is an excuse, and you know it." The valet shook his head. "It is the perfect reason to do it now."

Barr shook his head. "I'll see how things go as we move through the Christmastide season."

He hadn't taken a mistress because his children required care and supervision especially after his wife died, then life happened with both, and it had just been busy for the past several years. Truth be told, he'd been content with all the projects he'd put off when concentrating on his children. Occasionally over the years, he'd tryst with someone he met at a ball or other event, but those were few and far between. More often than not, if he had specific urges, he took himself in hand and left it at that. There were other things to occupy his mind, like the books in his library and the challenge of translating ancient texts or scrolls he came across at auctions merely for the fun of it.

Or he would wander the exhibits at the British Museum, walk through Hyde Park, visit lending libraries, all the while avoiding making eye contact with people.

"You are naught but a coward, Your Grace."

"Oh, I quite agree. My wife was the one who made social plans and dragged me out to them. Left to my own devices? I want no part of polite society."

"So you'll decay beneath this roof alongside your books and *objets d'art*, hmm?"

"I might, and will be happy to do so." Barr moved to a trunk near the back wall, covered with a layer of dust. "There is more to life than fucking one's brains out." In fact, there was much to be said about indulging in deep conversations, good debates, sharing private jokes, reading interesting bits to each other from a newspaper or a book, or simply sitting in silence while listening to the dratted rain.

"Now you sound like a man well beyond your years, and that is quite sad." The humor in Traver's voice tugged a grin from him.

"Bah." Ignoring his valet for the moment, Barr cracked open the trunk then rummaged through the contents. Thick tomes on a variety of dull subjects were what he unearthed. "Damn. It would appear my father's reading tastes were beyond boring, and I rather doubt he did much reading anyway." That just wasn't who his father was.

When one of the books slipped off the corner of the trunk where Barr had set it, it thudded to the wooden floor, but when the pages cracked open, he gawked, for the center of the book had been hollowed out. "What is this?" A slim volume with a faded yellow linen cover tumbled from the larger book. The cover was worn and aged, and the golden lettering on the front had all but flaked away, but from what was left, he discerned the title was a mix of Egyptian lettering and hieratic. "How interesting."

"It must be valuable if your father thought to hide it."

"Indeed." As Barr flipped delicately through the pages of text he couldn't understand, excitement buzzed at the base of his spine. "Quite a cheeky piece of literature." There were erotic drawings interspersed throughout the pages which provided a hint at the content. Some of them were quite explicit, almost as if it were an instruction manual for coupling written by Ancient Egyptians. A book of affection between lovers? He couldn't say until he could have it translated. "I'll wager this will fetch a princely sum at an auction house." He looked forward to poring over it in greater detail once he retrieved his reading spectacles, for the text was a bit blurry.

"You won't translate it?" Travers wished to know.

"I could, but I'm afraid Ancient Egyptian isn't my strength. It would take forever."

The valet nodded. "Or you could use the book for yourself. Perhaps it will give you a few ideas and encourage you to take a lover."

Heat sneaked up the back of Barr's neck. "Do shut up." Yet he couldn't help a grin. "I'd need it translated first before determining value… or reading it for pleasure."

"Or using it for pleasure," his friend was quick to add.

A huff left his throat. "Why must everything come down to bedding a woman?" Clearly, his valet had a healthy marriage.

"Intercourse and physical touch are vital parts of one's existence." Travers shrugged. "Honestly, you should move on to the next portion of your life, and you're a man who needs to be needed by a woman. No shame in it. Why not simply keep an open mind? It is the season of miracles, after all."

Barr couldn't help but briefly roll his eyes to the ceiling before resting his gaze on his friend. "Fine. Truce. If there comes a day when it doesn't rain, then I will seek out a woman for nothing more than to relieve carnal tensions. Would that suffice?"

It was a safe wager to offer, for he knew it would never stop raining; he'd be safe.

"Indeed, Your Grace." Travers beamed as he glanced about the space. "Let's catalogue some of these bits and bobs, see if we can sell it. Oh, and I'll bring the Christmas decorations down in the event you'll want to make use of them."

"I can't imagine that I will. My wife was the one who enjoyed decorating and entertaining during this time of year. Without her, it just seems… empty and a sacrilege to do so." He frowned at his valet. "However, do what makes you and your wife happy. I *have* missed the sparkle, though."

"As I said, you are a man who needs to be needed. Since you haven't had that in your life for a several years, you've fallen out of the habit of being social." Travers flicked his glance to the erotic book still in Barr's hand. "Perhaps in the course of finding someone to translate the book and then securing a buyer, you will stumble upon a connection that will help tug you back to the present." The valet's expression sobered. "The past, though lovely as it was, has nothing else to offer you."

Slowly, Barr nodded. "Perhaps you are correct." He looked at Travers. "Thank you for the reminder." As he tucked the small volume into the inside pocket of his jacket for later study, he sighed. "I'm not certain I even remember how to attract a woman." At least he was honest. "With my wife, it was easy, and it was such a long time ago." After twenty years of marriage, five more years since he'd lost her, it felt as if an age had gone by.

"Don't think too hard about it, Your Grace. Start with a

smile, perhaps a suggestive wink, or a play on words." Travers shrugged as he dug through boxes and trunks in the apparent search for Christmastide decorations. "The season will lend itself to cozy talks and the opportunity to act gentlemanly in the hopes of keeping a lady warm."

"I'll bear that in mind, my friend." Then he joined Travers at the trunk. "Let me help carry some of the boxes down for you. And tell your lovely wife she has the authority to use whatever of the staff she wishes to help with the decorations."

No matter that he was thoroughly alone for the first time in many years and wasn't inclined toward celebrations, that didn't mean everyone beneath the roof must suffer the same humbugs as he.

God help us all.

CHAPTER TWO

December 17, 1816
No 12 Hanover Square
Mayfair, London

MISS CATHERINE PICKWICK sat in her father's study, trying to make sense of his crabbed handwriting on his latest batch of notes as she attempted to transcribe them into an orderly outline. He was a professor at Cambridge in Ancient Roman studies and hoped to write a research paper while home during the Christmastide holidays, since he'd have no students to shepherd or keep an eye on, and no student work to mark up.

Frankly, she rather thought her father would research something until the day he died, for he found so much enjoyment in the process. At times, he would even forget the world around him in the hunt for knowledge.

Perhaps that was where she'd learned her love of books and manuscripts.

"Ah, there you are, Catherine."

She glanced up as her father came into the room. A barrel-chested man with thinning blond hair and a pair of half-moon spectacles perched often at the tip of his nose. Today he wore a brown tweed jacket that stretched across his shoulders and a brown velvet waistcoat that strained over his ever-widening stomach. The golden chain of his pocket watch glimmered in the candlelight.

"Good afternoon, Papa. I'd wondered where you'd gone."

"Just in from the Reading Room at the British Museum. I'm afraid I was engrossed in a few tomes there and lost track of the time." He came around the side of the desk and glanced at her progress. "I adore how your mind works. When you provide me outlines and talking points, writing papers or giving speeches come infinitely easier for me."

"Order sometimes allows more creativity." She rose from his chair to allow him to sit there. Instead, she settled into a leather chair across from the desk. "You should leave off with this for a bit. The Christmastide season will soon be upon us, and we both know how much you enjoy that."

She did as well, but it hadn't been the same since her mother died.

"I do. Right now, my mind is consumed with all things Roman." He gave her a wink. "In Roman times, the harsh British winter was split in half by the festival of Saturnalia, the midwinter date of the Julian Calendar. As the days grow colder and the nights draw close, our Christmas is something to look forward to in those bleak months. While the Christians of the world celebrate Christmas as the day of Jesus Christ's birth, this was not always the purpose of the holiday."

Cate nodded, for she'd heard the lecture many times before. "How interesting, Papa. Please continue." It fed her father's ego, and she tamped down a giggle as he warmed to his topic.

"It started as a farmer's religious festival to encourage and pray for the harvest of the coming year; its popularity grew and spread throughout the Roman Empire. This holiday break involved drinking, dancing, decorations, gifts and entertainment with family, friends, and neighbors." He opened an ornamental box on his desktop, removed a bit of snuff, then tamped it down into the ivory bowl of his pipe. "The festival of Saturnalia gave us the lighting of candles—called Cerei—and the idea of bringing evergreen tree boughs and branches indoors. In particular, the hiding of a silver sixpence in the Christmas pudding can be traced back to Roman times."

"Now that *is* interesting. You haven't added that point to this story before."

He grinned. "I like to see if you are paying attention at times." With another wink, he continued his tale. "The lucky Roman who discovered the hidden coin in the cake was then pronounced the lord or lady of the festival—*Saturnalicius princeps*—whose job it was to cause mischief and entertainment. The Roman invasion introduced Ancient Britain to these holiday traditions and now these familiar celebrations have filtered down throughout history, remaining long after the Christian conversion and even the collapse of the Ancient Roman Empire."

"Fascinating as always, Papa."

"Indeed." He nodded. "So you see, anyone who says Christmas is strictly a Christian holiday is much mistaken." Then he put the mouthpiece of his pipe between his lips, lit a match, set it to the snuff, and puffed a few times until it began to smolder. After extinguishing the match, he laid it into a small bowl in the tray where his pipe had rested. "Oh, and on the subject of Ancient Rome, I've come into possession of a couple of artifacts I bought from a farmer who'd unearthed buried Roman treasures on his farm a few years ago." Smoke drifted up to wreath his face. "I plan to present them to the British Museum should my paper be accepted by the Archeological Society of London."

"I'm so proud of you, Papa. Of course the paper will be accepted."

When he eased back in his chair, the springs protested. "I know you are, poppet, but I think we both know that I won't live forever." Wisps of smoke slowly curled toward the ceiling.

"Unfortunately." Cate sobered. "But now is not the time to talk of that."

"Or it's the perfect time." He shot her a speaking glance. "You are well past the age that grandchildren are possible…"

All gaiety fled. "Oh, please, not this again." Besides, it was humiliating, especially since the years had passed and there was nothing she could do about it. "I always thought I had the time to let a man court me and then to marry, perhaps travel the world before having children, but..." She shrugged. No sense in mourning for something she'd never truly lost. "I filled my days with other things. There is no shame in it."

"I well know the feeling." Her father chuckled. Pipe smoke continued to drift and pool in clouds at the ceiling. "People like us gain satisfaction from knowledge and studying and the ancient world when we should pay attention to the modern one."

Slowly, she nodded. "Mama warned me about just this. I should have listened, especially since part of my time was taken up with being a governess." Twice. To horrible, spoiled children. Even now it made her shiver.

"Yet you are nine and thirty, poppet. It's time to have love in your life, to experience that at least once."

"Ha." She snorted. "Love was how I landed into trouble before."

Oh, God, how she'd courted trouble and scandal. Was it her fault she'd been hired by handsome men to instruct their broods? Where she'd delighted in teaching geography, Latin, and cultures from other societies all over the world, her first employer had delighted in seducing her one rainy night when his wife had gone visiting her sister in Surrey and she'd taken the children. Cate had been young and naïve and didn't want to say no to an earl, but that was no excuse.

She might have lost her innocence, but knowledge was knowledge, and she took to bed sport with alacrity and enthusiasm. That had been a glorious week... until the lady of the house had come home and the servants tattled.

As expected, Cate had been sacked with references, though, because the woman had been a student of her father's.

The second incident was just as much of a disaster, only this time it was she who'd done the seducing, for the ambassador had worn spectacles, and they were a weakness of hers. That affair had lasted six months, for he was often away from London, but eventually, it was he who'd let her go because of guilt and the betrayal of his wife.

As well as a pregnancy scare on her part that hadn't amounted to anything.

After she lost the second governess position, she'd gone to work at a lending library. Books were never disappointing and never caused heartbreak or incurred a betrayal of her body.

And so the years had passed.

Her father chuckled. "Neither of those times were love, my girl. Merely lust."

"We'll never know, but they were quite confusing and messy. I thought myself in love with the ambassador, at least."

"Life is quite like that." He frowned then rested his pipe on the plate. "I would like to see you at least on the path of being courted by the year's end, my dear. Humor an old man."

"But…"

"You are my only child, and I want your future settled, to have the kind of union your mother and I shared. There is nothing like having that special person at your side, who truly understands you, and you rub on well together through all corners of life."

Her parents' union had been a beautiful thing. "Dear Papa, don't worry. I possess enough charm that I can completely enchant a man if one comes my way who proves moderately interesting this Christmastide season." She came around his desk and placed a kiss on the top of his balding head. "I'll remind you again, I won't marry unless there is love. Anything else is a waste of time."

Was her parents' union too hard to achieve? She didn't know, but it was a goal. Then she glanced at the time piece suspended on a gold chain around her neck. On the other side of the watch face was a small mirror. "Oh, heavens, I need to scoot. I'm working the afternoon shift at the lending library, but I should be home for dinner."

"Try not to get drowned with the rain." Though we waved her away, he was already engrossed in his notes.

AS IT TURNED out, it was quite a busy day at the library, where she'd helped returning patrons as well as new ones find books they were compatible with and interested in.

Located in a quiet cul-de-sac off Fleet Street, Edgerton's Lending Library was an oasis from the world. The large central room featured two floor-to-ceiling windows at the front, while the three sides of the room were lined with tall, wooden shelves filled with books. Some on the upper shelves were only accessed by wooden ladders. Off to one side of the library room was a reading room, where patrons could go to read the books they didn't wish to take home in silence. Conversation was discouraged in that room. Off the other side of the library was a lounge, where tea was often served and patrons could socialize within reason.

The whole space uplifted Cate's spirits, and by and large she enjoyed working alongside her male librarians.

Today, there were two librarians in addition to her working at either circulation desk. As she chatted with one of the ladies inquiring about a specific book they didn't have, Cate's attention was diverted when a man entered the lending library, with looks that were quite arresting.

"Oh!" The whispered exclamation was enough to catch her patron's attention, who glanced over her shoulder and also stared at the newcomer.

"He is lovely, isn't he?" the patron whispered back, clearly forgetting about books for the moment.

"Yes." She couldn't help but stare, for the man was broad-shouldered with a commanding presence. Easily she could imagine him being sun-kissed... if London ever saw the sun again. Piercing blue eyes seemed to see everything at once, dark hair beneath the brim of his top hat glimmered with silver strands. Oddly, she had the feeling he would rather be anywhere than mingling with society, perhaps training horses or doing something with his hands.

Mmm, did he have callouses on those hands? Difficult to tell, for he wore dove gray kid gloves that matched the color of his greatcoat.

As he strode to one of the circulation desks, Cate followed his progress with her gaze. Then she realized she recognized him— the Duke of Scarborough, one of the patrons of her library as well as a couple of others throughout London, who always made donations yearly in his dead wife's name.

A nervous flutter moved through her veins. "If you will excuse me?" she murmured to the patron she'd been speaking with, but before she could make her way to the duke, one of the male clerks rushed over and asked if he could assist.

"I would have no idea, since I don't know your qualifications," the duke said, and even across the room like she was, the rumble of his voice tickled through her chest. "I would like to speak to someone who can give me a recommendation for someone who can translate an Ancient Egyptian text."

The young clerk's expression fell; it seemed he wouldn't be able to assist the duke. "That is certainly not me, Your Grace, but I can make inquiries. One moment."

What a novice. And something that one should never tell a duke. When he rushed off, Cate slowly approached the man, and oh, dear, he towered over her by at least seven inches. To be fair, she was only a few inches above five feet, so practically everyone was taller than she. "Perhaps I can help, Your Grace."

"Oh?" A light of interest appeared in his sapphire eyes. "Why do you think so?"

Ah, a bit of arrogance. It would be lovely fun to disabuse him of that. "My father is a crack researcher of ancient cultures, both professionally and personally. He has many friends and colleagues who are scholars, adventurers, and linguists, and among them they delve deep into Egyptian cultures and languages."

He nodded. "And?"

A huff escaped her. "Throughout my formative years, I used

to sneak into Papa's library during those evenings. Hidden behind doors or window drapes, I'd listen to them for hours. Once found out, my father, instead of consigning me to my room, gave me a stack of books, introduced me to those men, and allowed me to study at my own pace to my heart's content."

"How interesting." His eyes reflected that. "Everything Egyptian is a developing subject within academic circles, mainly kept to the men's clubs and whatnot."

"It was… still is, for research never ceases and knowledge is always moving forward." She shrugged. "Learning such shouldn't only be kept to one sex. It's fascinating, besides."

"Now you've piqued my personal interest."

"Ah." The crisp, clean scent of him threatened to drown her. "Perhaps you'll come with me to the lounge? We can speak more privately there."

"Of course."

The reading room would be full at this hour, but the lounge, though crowded during teatime, had more privacy because people could converse at tables or sofas.

When they settled at a small table near a window where the rain slashed against the glass, she introduced herself. "Good afternoon. I'm Miss Pickwick, and I can read hieroglyphs as well as some Hieratic. I might be of assistance, or I might not, but my father is a professor at Cambridge. Studying the ancient world has always been in my life."

"Ah, excellent." He nodded. Drops of rain dotted the shoulders of his greatcoat as well as his top hat. "I'm Scarborough."

Oh, I am well aware. The heat of him fairly reached out and grabbed her, and the sound of his voice sent delicious shivers over her skin. She gave him a smile. "Did you bring the text?"

"I did not. It's at home in a safe since it's quite old. The linen cover is crumbling in places."

"Fair enough. Can you describe it?"

"Of course." He lowered his voice, but that only made it more thrilling. "I found the slim volume in the hollowed-out pages of another book, not even on the same subject, so someone obviously wished it to remain hidden, either because of its age or its content."

"Oh? How so?" Already, the story was fascinating.

"It's some sort of Egyptian poetry, but I rather believe it's an erotic love story following the journey of a couple. Or so I assume."

She frowned. "Why do you think that?"

"It's a delicate subject matter. Are you sure you wish to know?" When she nodded, he continued. A hint of ruddy color rose above his cravat. "There are drawings throughout that are quite graphic and of sexual positions."

"I see." Heat seeped into her cheeks. "Perhaps you should ask for a male reference, then. You might be more comfortable during the translation." For it might prove scandalous. "Best wishes." When she rose to leave, he grabbed her wrist, his fingers tight and surprising on her arm. Swift tingles jumped up her limb to her elbow.

"Please sit down, Miss Pickwick." His intense gaze roved over her face. "Can you give me a translation expert off the top of your head?"

"No, but I—"

"Then why *shouldn't* I hire you?"

Her heartbeat skittered into a fast rhythm. "For one, I'm unmarried. It would be a scandalous endeavor unless I bring a maid or companion."

The duke shook his head. "I'm afraid I don't want extra company, for I'd like to keep the book a secret until I decide what to do with it."

"Fair enough." She nodded, but couldn't think of anything else erudite to say.

"I can promise you're in no danger of being molested."

Well, that's disappointing.

"Ah, because I'm clearly an old spinster? How rude." She hadn't meant to say that aloud, and to a duke no less, but it couldn't be helped.

A faint grin tugged at the corners of his sensual mouth. "No, because this arrangement would be strictly business, of course."

Insanity went through her brain, which stole her ability to remain professional. "Mmm, you don't think you're attractive to women, then?"

His flush darkened. "That didn't occur to me."

"Very well. I shall promise you the same."

He frowned. "Meaning what?"

"That you won't be molested by me." And she winked. *What was wrong with her?* "When and where should I come to assess the text?"

For long moments, he rested his intense gaze on her while a shiver shot down her spine. "Tomorrow, if it's convenient, at my townhouse." Immediately, he gave her a calling card. "The day after if it's not. Unless in doing so I'm taking you away from Christmastide planning."

She couldn't help but chuckle. "You are not. My father is occupied with writing a paper, so this is favorable; I don't work at the lending library tomorrow."

"Ah, excellent. Shall we say around two o'clock? We could share tea once you are finished."

"Jolly good." Then she frowned. "Though I'm not certain my assessment or translation can be wrapped up in a few hours." Then she stood, for if she lingered in his company for too much longer, she'd become a silly widgeon. The duke rose to his feet as well. "I look forward to working with you, Your Grace."

"Remember, no companion or maid. I believe we don't require supervision, and I don't want word of this find getting out."

"Of course." Was he odd or merely careful?

"Thank you. Then I shall see you tomorrow, Miss Pickwick." With a nod, he exited the lounge, and she peered after him.

Good heavens. When her knees would no longer support her, Cate sat back down on her chair. How was she supposed to translate a book if the mere presence of him in a lending library had her reacting like a schoolgirl with her first crush?

Or worse?

CHAPTER THREE

December 18, 1816
Combes House
Grosvenor Square, Mayfair
London

O F COURSE IT was raining, for when didn't it?

Barr clasped his hands behind his back as he stared out the drawing room windows. Would Miss Pickwick arrive today as she'd said? He frowned that the raindrops on the glass. It had been fate or luck when he'd met her at the lending library yesterday, and there had been an odd and immediate connection between them he couldn't explain.

That provoked an even greater frown. Why? He didn't know her and had never met her before yesterday, but her academic experience level was impressive.

Movement from the street caught his eye and wrenched him from his thoughts. A closed carriage stopped at the curb. Once the driver climbed down, he came around and opened the door, put down the steps, and then assisted a woman out. She hitched her navy skirts up to avoid the mud and puddles, which afforded him a quick glimpse of a brown half-boot. A matching navy pelisse covered most of her form, and a plain navy-dyed straw bonnet hid her hair and face from his view. Both would protect her from the ever-present rain.

When she came up the short walkway to the townhouse, he

lost sight of her, but excitement buzzed at the base of his spine. She had kept her promise, and it took every ounce of his willpower to remain where he was instead of rushing to the ground floor prematurely.

Eventually, his butler arrived at the drawing room door.

"Your Grace, there is a Miss Pickwick here. She says she has been invited by you to look at a rare book?" The butler's tone suggested it could possibly be a lie. He was a man of indeterminate age and looks, the type of man one would forget immediately after passing him in the street. Perhaps that was a good thing in his position. "I have put her in the library until I checked with you."

"Thank you, Withers. I did, indeed, invite her, but please use discretion. She will come by every day until the text is translated."

"Of course, Your Grace." Then he left the room.

A ripple of anxiety crossed Barr's nerves. Why the hell was he anxious? She was here to translate a book. Nothing more, yet the teasing words they'd exchanged briefly yesterday, as well as the glances rife with interest, couldn't discount the immediate and electric desire crackling between them in that lounge.

Perhaps it had been naught but a fluke.

With a tug to the bottom of his jacket, he made his way downstairs to the library. At the door, he paused, merely to study her while she perused the books on the shelves.

Brown hair the color of coffee had been upswept in what seemed like a careless bun, but there was enough thickness and volume in those tresses to make him suspect it tended to naturally curl. A slender neck gave away to slight shoulders, a nipped-in waist and then rounded hips. She was short, more than several inches from his height, and he remembered by experience that the top of her head stood at his shoulder.

As he came further into the comforting space, he softly cleared his throat. "Good afternoon, Miss Pickwick. Lovely to see you again."

When she turned about with a book in her hands, she offered

a tentative smile. "Hullo, Your Grace." Curiosity lit the depths of her rich, brown eyes. "I hope you don't mind that I was browsing your titles."

"I do not. It's good to have someone find interest in them besides me." He flicked his gaze up and down her person. The plain, navy day dress did nothing for her figure, nor did it enhance her modest bosom. When he snapped his focus back to her face, one of her dark eyebrows rose in question. "Uh, shall we get right to it? Er…" He coughed. "I meant to the translation." Would she assume something else? Heat went up the back of his neck. "I'm sorry, that was crass and rude. Forgive me. I have been out of polite society for a bit."

"As well as speaking simple words?" Teasing threaded through her tone.

"So it seems." Why did she have the power to render him stupid?

"Put yourself at ease, Your Grace." Her smile was both enigmatic and slightly arousing, with the bottom lip slightly fuller than the upper one. "Why don't we spend a bit of time talking? Share about ourselves. Then I will be more familiar with you and your life and how the book fits into that."

"Of course. I appreciate that." As she replaced the book she held onto the shelf, he began his story. "I'm the father of two grown children. My son is six and twenty, and newly married. Currently, he resides at Scarborough Hall near Cornwall with his new bride, as well as my aging mother."

"Oh, my. That can't be fun, or convenient, for the newlywed couple."

"It can't be helped with the weather." Barr shrugged as he paced the length of the room in front of the longest bookshelf. "The boy took on the responsibility without complaint. He has quite a head for business, even this young, and has made some rather impressive investments. Besides, Mother doesn't like living in London. Says it's too loud, too crowded, and too dirty."

"She's not wrong." Miss Pickwick trailed to one of the shorter shelves on one side of the room where a wooden ladder rested. "And just now? It's far too wet."

What would it take to make her exactly that? A bit of wicked bedeviling on that very ladder? He covered his shock at his own thoughts by uttering a forced cough. *What the devil is wrong with me?*

When she glanced at him with concern, he shook his head. "My daughter, meanwhile, is two and twenty. She's staying with her cousins in Derbyshire. My sister and her brood will keep the girl busy and happy until the roads are passable." For a few moments, he paused. "I have high hopes for Abigail. Her mother wanted her to marry well."

"Ah." His guest stared at him as if she were trying to figure him out. "And you? What do *you* want for her?"

"Honestly? I want her to be happy." In the end, that is all he wanted for every member of his family. "Life is already difficult for women in this world. Wedding the wrong man shouldn't be part of it, so I'm not going to force the issue. I'll let her try whatever she wishes. Marriage will come or it won't. It's her decision."

Surprise etched through Miss Pickwick's expression. "That's a good attitude to have, and it will give your daughter a taste of freedom. She'll use you to measure potential suitors."

"Is that a good thing?"

"Yes." When she once more smiled, his gaze dropped to her mouth. What would those lips feel like beneath his? "It is. You seem like a sensible man who doesn't tolerate his time being wasted, and I'll wager you have a work ethic and morals. This will go a long way into helping your daughter choose a husband."

"Thank you. I try." He once more clasped his hands behind his back, and he drifted closer to her. "Is that what you've done? Held your father up as a model?"

"A bit, I suppose. My father is lovely. When he took his post at Cambridge, I was so proud of him. He'd finally come into his own after years of writing papers and researching, as well as poking about tombs and ruins." Her eyes took on a faraway look. "I always thought I'd follow in his footsteps and travel the world, but I'm more comfortable ensconced in libraries."

"Some of the loveliest libraries in the world are, sadly, not in England."

"I know." She lowered her voice to a teasing whisper. "Traveling by boat makes me ill."

"Ah." What a delightful admission. "Is that why you've never married?" What a nodcock he was. "I meant not finding someone who lives up to your father's disciplines, not being sick on a ship."

"No at all. Unfortunately, I let myself become lost in my studies, in books, in literature, in everything that interested me and kept my mind engaged. It was a lovely way to occupy my time, and he never denied me books or the opportunities to learn new things." Another grin, and this one went straight to his stones. "When I came up for air, I was surprised so much time had passed and that I was so old."

"You hardly look ancient."

She chuckled. "Thank you. I'm nine and thirty. So far on the shelf I'm collecting dust." She shrugged and the gesture pulled her bodice taut over her breasts. "There were men here and there over the years who showed interest."

"No offers?"

"Not ones that weren't scandalous."

He frowned even as his pulse increased a tick. "What happened? That is, unless it's too much like prying for me to ask?"

"Like much of what I study, it's ancient history." She waved a hand in dismissal. "Some of the potential suitors weren't amused when my time and attention was divided. Some of them outright demanded that I give up the 'nonsense' of reading and poring over translations, for, as they said, that wasn't what women were created for, while still others… Well, I suppose I'm a bit vain, for their looks did nothing for me. My mother always said if there weren't at least flutters early on, then a man simply wasn't worth the effort."

Fascinating insight. "I take it your parents married for love?"

"Oh yes. They were so sweet together. Always giggling and holding hands, brushing up against each other as they moved past each other, spending time together in and out of the bedroom." A pink blush stained her cheeks. How lovely! "Mama gardened while Papa wrote papers and translated ancient texts. In fact, he taught me that skill. My father loved her until she drew her last breath from complications of pneumonia six years ago. Occasionally, grief sneaks up and knocks into me. I miss her." She frowned, and his attention once more went to her mouth.

"I think that's why I bury myself in work, so those feelings aren't as acute. The smell of books, the feel of them, the sound of the pages turning brings me comfort."

"I know exactly what you mean, on both counts." He paused as he thought over his next words. "I lost my wife years ago, and time now moves strangely. There are days when it goes up and down in the same period." When Miss Pickwick nodded, he continued. "I'll wager your father loves her still," he said quietly, for he knew what it felt like to not have a spouse in his life. "Those feelings don't evaporate. I think we just learn how to make room for them, so they don't take over our lives."

"No doubt he does, but I wouldn't mind if he chose to seek out a new companion. He needs that; we all do. Being alone takes a toll, I think."

Did that mean she was on the hunt for a husband? Shaking his head slightly to clear the thoughts, Barr said, "He probably won't until your future is settled. That's what good fathers do."

"Hmm." Her lips turned downward in a frown. "I hadn't thought of it like that, but then yesterday he impressed upon me that I should marry. As if I could go to a shop and pick out a decent man. I wish it were that simple."

"Then perhaps you should choose an indecent man," he quipped, as an odd sense of humor came over him.

"I beg your pardon?" Her confusion was both adorable and somehow lit fires in his blood.

"You said finding a decent man wasn't simple. Perhaps locating an indecent one would be easier."

"Ah." Her smile was slow but addictive. What would those lips feel like against his... or better, wrapped around his engorged length? *Good God, man, rein yourself in.*

Then common sense came back to take control. Barr shrugged. "I apologize for the risqué comment."

"It is no bother. I welcome a break from the ordinary, actually." Amusement danced in the dark depths of her eyes. "I'm no stranger to scandal. I suppose I *should* mention that before this position begins. You might not wish to be associated with me after that."

Now that *was* intriguing. "How so?"

She wandered to another bookshelf. "Before being a librarian, I was a governess. A failed one, since I was turned out both times for becoming intimately involved with my employers." Another blush, but a bit more faint. "It doesn't matter how those liaisons came about."

"I see." His chest was tight, not with worry, but from jealousy, of the men she'd been with. Then he berated himself, for he knew her not at all. "I suppose I can't fault you. You are quite lovely."

"Ha, such gammon." She waved his comment away. "Do stop, Your Grace. Looks have nothing to do with desire or passion. Such a connection can happen between two people regardless." One of her dark eyebrows rose. "Also, I take exception to society's acceptance of men having trysts, but when a woman does it—unless she's a widow—she is condemned by those same eyes."

From the moment they'd begun conversing, she'd proved herself quite intelligent. "That is so true." The elusive scent of her perfume teased his nose with floral notes and a hint of vanilla and something he couldn't identify but compelled him to move closer. "Oh, and by the by, I don't wish for us to be formal while working on this project. You may use my title—Scarborough—or call me Barrington, which is my Christian name, or even just Barr. That's what my friends call me when not using the title." What a long-winded explanation for a very pedestrian thing.

For a long time, Miss Pickwick stared at him, searched his face with her gaze for God only knew, but he hoped she found it within him. Finally, she nodded. "I rather like the name Barrington. One doesn't hear that much. It makes you unique and memorable."

He released the breath he hadn't realized he'd been holding. "Thank you."

"I'm Catherine, or Cate, since only my father calls me the by full name."

"It's lovely." Soon, he'd make a fool of himself by chasing that perfume in the air. In the end, perhaps he wasn't in control of his own life. Perhaps it was fate that moved his feet, for he apparently was well on his way to losing his mind—at least temporarily—because he leaned toward her, put a crooked finger beneath her chin, tipped up her head, then gently pressed his lips to hers. Surprise jumped into her eyes as she held his gaze. His pulse hammered in his ears as he waited, stunned. He hadn't been with any woman let alone kissed one since his last tryst, which seemed an age ago. Would she slap his face, and rightly so? He eased back a few inches to see what she would do, she gave him a tiny nod, so with even more shock knocking about his brain, he moved his hand to cup her cheek and kissed her again, this time with more stick.

Tongues crashed and dueled. Silk slid against satin. Her lips cradled his while he slowly moved over hers in exploration. One of her hands came to rest on his chest, her fingers curling softly into his lapel. And when she kissed him back, heat slipped into his bloodstream and interest shivered into his shaft.

That brought back pieces of his sanity, and he pulled away with a gasp, remembering who he was and why she was here. Tugging on the knot of his cravat, he said, "My apologies. I don't know what came over me."

A giggle escaped her, and the sound did nothing to relieve the sudden tightness in his groin. Amusement twinkled in her eyes, along with a subtle darkening. Had she felt that inexplicable pull too? "Oh, I'll wager I do. It happens to all of us." As Miss Pickwick scooted back and put a bit of distance between them, she touched her lips with a fingertip. Was she assessing the skill of the kiss? Remembering it? Did she wish the embrace had been longer?

Why the devil did he want to know?

"Your talent in kissing aside…" A heavy sigh followed. "Perhaps we should move to the purpose of my coming here before things grow wildly out of hand."

"Right." At least he had his answer. She thought he had talent. That was good to know, and it buoyed his ego slightly. *Why the hell did I kiss her?* And perhaps more to the point, why did that one kiss not satisfy him in the least? "Let me just fetch the book." Could she see his erection through his charcoal-colored breeches? Damn, how embarrassing. One would think him a randy youth, but he couldn't help it. There was something about her he apparently couldn't resist.

"I would appreciate it." Once she seated herself on a low leather sofa with a high back, she glanced about the room. "If you don't mind, each day I intend to take a break from the translation by going through your books. I'm always interested in seeing different collections in the hopes I'll find a book that will send me down another rabbit hole of research."

"You are more than welcome." Willing his body to settle, Barr moved to a small cabinet at the other side of the room. Opening a slim drawer, he removed the volume in question, then closed the drawer. "My father amassed quite the collection though he wasn't genuinely fond of reading. I think he merely liked collecting them."

"While there's nothing wrong with that, I would rather delve into the pages and lose myself in the words."

"Indeed." Just when he thought he'd sorted himself, the moment he sat next to her on the sofa, and the warmth and scent of her reached out to him, he was in danger—again—of making a cake of himself. "Regardless, here is the book. There are thin cotton gloves on the table over there if you'd rather make use of them."

And he placed the book in her hands with the distinct thought that it wasn't just the Egyptian volume he was giving her.

CHAPTER FOUR

*G*OOD HEAVENS BUT *Scarborough is quite potent, even from one little kiss.*

"For the moment, gloves aren't necessary but will be once I begin work on the translation." How amazing it was to hold a book that had survived centuries! The yellow color of the linen cover had faded, of course, and was crumbling at the corners and a bit on the spine. Some of the gold lettering had flaked away. "How astonishing."

"I thought so, too. The thought that something this old has been hidden away in this very townhouse?" The duke shook his head. "And now it's seeing the light of day again?" A sound of awe escaped him. "Incredible."

"Agreed." Carefully and with gentle fingertips, Cate looked through the book, pausing here and there on a few pages. "It's interesting they used colors for some of the drawings." The red had faded to the color of brown dried blood, while some of the blues and greens were quite muted but still beautiful. True, some of the more graphic drawings put heat in her cheeks, but she was anxious to translate the text. "I'm sure it's a wonderful book, whatever the subject."

And she admitted to herself that experimenting with some of the positions indicated within the pages would be quite exhilarating and exciting.

"Would you have any idea of how old the book is?"

"Oh, well, look at this cartouche." She pointed to the drawing at the top of one of the pages:

"This is the name of Akhenaten. Some have said he was a heretic and a revolutionary, the world's first 'individual', and his reign—known as the Amarna period—is vigorously studied and debated. Will probably still be hundreds of years from now." She shrugged, and then settled into the familiarity of the subject matter. "Shall I continue?"

"Yes, please." When he removed a pair or round spectacles from his interior jacket pocket and then popped them on the end of his nose as he looked at the inscription, flutters went through her lower belly, for a man with spectacles was another of her weaknesses.

Shoving that thought away, Cate went on. "Akhenaten was a pharaoh of the 18th Dynasty. Before he gave himself that name, however, he had been Amenhotep IV, son of the great Amenhotep III, who—along with the female pharaoh Hatshepsut a century earlier—made this period a golden age for Egypt."

"This is all so fascinating," he said in a lowered voice as he traced the cartouche with a fingertip. "And to think we're gazing upon the same parchment as people of that period."

She nodded. "From all accounts or theories—and do bear in mind this could all just be speculation or stories until we definitely know the truth—his wife was Nefertiti and one of his children the boy king, Tutankhamun. Though all of this, of course, is argued between scholars and archeologists." A sigh escaped, for she wished she were out in the field. "Akhenaten reigned from 1353 to 1336 BC, although as with everything in Ancient Egypt, there are doubts and uncertainty until more relics and tombs are discovered."

"Imagine being on a dig like that, finding something that will definitively change our knowledge of the world."

"It has long been a dream of mine, actually." Then she frowned as she turned another page in the book. "When his older brother died, he assumed rule where he continued his father's building projects, worshipped the usual gods, married had children. After only a few years on the throne, Amenhotep IV celebrated his sed festival, a form of jubilee normally reserved for a pharaoh's 30th year. According to some scholars, in his fifth year, he rejected the chief deity of the pantheon, Amun, in favor of the Aten. Unlike the other gods, the Aten was not anthropomorphic but depicted as a solar disk shining down rays with hands at the ends."

"And he instructed all to worship one god," the duke said as he held her gaze with fascination shining in the blue depths. "That must have caused an uproar."

"Perhaps in some circles. Change is difficult no matter the century. To show his loyalty to the Aten with the particular cult or religion who held power throughout the land, Amenhotep changed his name to Akhenaten—meaning some variation of beneficial to the Aten—and announced his intention to build a new capital. After, he moved the religious center of Egypt from Thebes. By his ninth year, Akhenaten made unprecedented radical steps to establish his religion—he proscribed the old gods entirely, declaring the Aten to be the *only* god. For this, he has been described as one of the first to institute monotheism. Everything changed under his reign, and I can only guess that made him a target to those subjects who dissented."

The duke nodded. "Power and politics were always changing in Egypt. The area, for centuries, was always held in the grip of such struggles."

"Still is, if you truly think about it." Carefully, Cate closed the book. "This was perhaps written for the pharaoh or his wife, or the pharaoh and a mistress, perhaps even designated to be left in his tomb for the afterlife. Since his tomb hasn't been found yet, this is, of course, speculation on my part, and even then, no one would believe any theories if they come from a woman. And the questions of why this book was left out of a tomb is still a large one." She frowned. "I don't even know if this was supposed to be for a tomb."

He huffed. "Poppycock. Women are perfectly capable of having intelligence and learning things on every subject, truth be told." He tapped the book still sitting in her lap. "Perhaps he commissioned the book for a second, younger wife?"

"Could be, depending on how that particular society was structured." She shrugged, and when she did, her shoulder brushed his chest leaving heated tingles behind. "Age doesn't mean a woman wouldn't be interested in trying new things or wouldn't embrace adventurous carnal activities. From everything we're learning about Ancient Egypt, we're discovering they were quite progressive and open with sexual congress. For them, it was merely another way of expressing themselves through affection. Not like the scandal it is apparently now."

Interesting, that, how society became more prudish as time went on.

"Ah." Scarborough's eyes darkened slightly. "That is quite true. My wife was interested in such things until she was too ill and too weak." When a tiny waver entered his voice, her chest tightened in sympathy. "I'll admit, the longer a person is with another, said relations have a tendency to grow… stale even if the couple enjoys each other."

As surprise gripped her, Cate's eyebrows rose. "Perhaps, but I'll wager the act is that much sweeter because of the familiarity."

"At times."

Such a scandalous topic of discussion. How did things like this happen to her? She flicked her gaze over his form. What must he look like *sans* clothing? That first kiss they'd shared, impromptu as it was, lit fires in her blood she couldn't ignore. A throb of heat went through her, something she hadn't known for far too long. *Why* had he done it? And more to the point, would he do it again?

"My father tells me it's folly to connect with men on that

level, that I should keep myself aloof and let someone court me, because that is what society demands."

Silence reigned between them for a handful of seconds, then the duke nodded.

"What do *you* think?"

No one had ever asked her that before. Warm pleasure went through her chest as she shrugged. "I can discover far more about a man through carnal acts than I can with months of verbal conversation or drives about Town. I'm afraid I'm not the type of woman to cool my heels, waiting on a man for anything. I've always thought if he can't make up his mind about me and a possible future together within a few weeks or so, then he's not for me." Her cheeks burned at the blunt admission. "I shouldn't have said that, so if you'd like to find a different translator, I'll understand."

Would the actions from her past and her candid way of speaking hinder this new position?

"Bah." He held her gaze with his own. "We should be allowed to utter our truths, regardless of rank or society's rules or subject matter. I appreciate the fact you feel comfortable enough in my company to share." Then he removed his spectacles and placed them on a nearby table.

"Thank you." In some relief, Cate nodded, and again focused on one of the pages in the slim volume. "Upon initial inspection, the ancient language is flowery with a cadence of poetic prose; a veritable love letter from a man to a woman."

"Interesting."

"Indeed." She turned the book over in her hands, but there was nothing inscribed on the back cover. "In many ways, as someone who studies ancient cultures and skips through history in the books I read, eavesdropping, as it were, around the great love affairs from movers and shakers makes me feel like an outcast, since I can never make a relationship go the distance."

"Not necessarily."

She frowned. "How so?" Why she admitted these very deep

secrets to a veritable stranger, she couldn't fathom.

"On the contrary, it makes you compelling and interesting. It matters not what your past relationships have consisted of." His gaze flicked from the book to her face, and those intense blue pools threatened to drag her under, made even more compelling when he scooted a tad bit closer to her on the sofa. "Forbidden words in that book or not, your future is yours to build how you wish."

A queer sort of squeeze went through her heart. "What a lovely thing to say." It was difficult to discern which of them moved first, but one moment she was sitting there, looking at him, and in the next, Cate was in his arms with his mouth on hers, and he encouraged her to lie backward on the soft leather of the sofa. The book of poetry and prose slipped off her lap to tumble to the Aubusson carpet, unheeded.

Good heavens, what was this quick and strong attraction between them? And God help her, she didn't want to resist. In fact, she encouraged the duke's overture, for his kisses were sublime and she wished to see how far he would go. Was he a gentleman or could he rise to a rogue if given the proper motivation? When he slipped a hand beneath her hip and another beneath her head, Cate's eyes fluttered closed as she reveled in the feel of his body over hers and his lips moving on hers.

Why am I so taken in by the strong, hard feel of a man's body?

The scent of his cologne teased her nose, the softness of the hair at his nape, the electric glide of the tip of his tongue along the seam of her lips all worked to usher her toward an undoing of sorts. Her hands drifted to his cravat and quickly loosened the knot, and a sigh of utter bliss escaped her.

I suppose I'm always destined to be embroiled in scandal.

"This is insanity," he whispered against her lips, but there was a slight hesitation as he cupped her breasts through the fabric of her dress.

"Perhaps, but it is also undeniable." She urged him onward, for that tension between them needed clearing before they could go forward with anything.

"It's maddening, but that doesn't mean I'm above exploring it." As he spoke, the duke resituated them both so that they reclined on their sides with him wedged behind her between the high back of the sofa and her. "Yet, I shouldn't…"

The rumble of his voice in her ear sent shivers scudding over her skin. "Because it's exploiting our working relationship or because you are a widower?" Daring much, she took his hand and placed it over one of her breasts.

He followed unspoken instructions wonderfully well, for he slipped his fingers inside her bodice, and the second he brushed those digits over her nipple, the bud pebbled. Sensations zipped through her that made her gasp. "Perhaps a bit of both."

Words escaped her at that moment, for the more he bedeviled the tip, the more waves of heated need swept over her. When he left off to ease that same hand beneath her skirting and skimmed his palm over the outside of her thigh, a sigh left her throat. The callouses on his fingertips and palm spoke to labor, and that made her even more curious.

But before she could ask him about what he did to create them, he put a knee between her thighs, and then he took full advantage by easing his hand through the curls hiding her sex. "Scarborough… Barr… I… Ooh…"

That was the moment he encouraged the button at her center out of hiding and he brushed a fingertip over that nubbin. He shifted position again so he could play with her other nipple with his free hand, and as he did that, he fit his other hand more tightly against her sensitive flesh. She put her hand atop his, guiding him to where she wanted him, and he did such an admirable job of applying various bits of friction to her swollen button that her eyes soon crossed from the flood of sensations.

"What sort of hold do you have over me that I've known you less than an hour, and here I am, violating your body like this?" Confusion and desire graveled his voice as his breath warmed the side of her neck.

"I don't know." Her breaths came in pants, for she could hardly concentrate on anything but his fingers on her button and nipple, sliding, stroking, circling, rubbing. "But it's caught me in its grip as well."

He didn't answer with words. Instead, he applied himself with bedeviling that nubbin to within an inch of its life.

Unrelenting pressure stacked and built within her, searching for an outlet. She moved her hips in time to his, and there was no mistaking how interested he was, for the hard evidence of his desire pressed into the curve of her arse.

"Oh... Barr!"

Faster his fingers worked, and before she knew what was happening, that release broke over her and she was pitched over the edge with a galloping heartbeat and heat dancing over her skin. When she inhaled to cry out her completion, he leaned close and took the utterance into himself with a kiss. Relief shuddered through her, for she didn't want the servants rushing in.

As she came back down to Earth, she gave into a shiver and relaxed in his hold. "For a man who says he hasn't done this recently, I'd say that showing was quite something." In fact, her words were still rather breathless.

"Ha." But he grinned and then lifted off her. "I appreciate the praise."

"Wait." Not ready to give up the closeness of him, Cate reached for the waist of his breeches. "Let me return the favor." And it would allow her to have a look at him. From the bulge that had pressed against her backside as he'd pleasured her, he would be magnificent.

"I'm afraid I'll have to thwart you in that endeavor," he said with a surprising wink as he left the sofa. "That *was* a bit of insanity, though."

"It was." As if he'd dumped a bucket of water on her, ardor cooled, and she came back to her senses. Surprise mixed with residual satisfaction as she righted herself and tidied her clothing. It was all quite odd, for she hadn't encountered a man who'd made such an impression on her so quickly, and certainly not one she had allowed such intimate access to her body like that. Still, she gained her feet, though her knees were a trifle weak. The two times in the past when she allowed her body to make decisions for her instead of her brain hadn't worked out well.

So why had she done it again with the duke? It couldn't happen again, not even for academic research and interest. Did she want to ruin yet another friendship and paying position by repeating the same habits?

"Forgive me for this, Scarborough." Cate held up a hand, palm outward. "We need to put forth some rules before we start." Did she refer to the work she'd been commissioned to do or something far more pleasurable?

"Fair enough and I agree." He retreated to the nearest bookshelf and leaned and shoulder against it then crossed his arms at his chest. "Regardless of what's between us, this connection that burns like fire and flows like lightning, I refuse to take advantage of you or the work I've asked you to do."

Slowly, she nodded. "What if I wish to do that with you?" Why couldn't she control her tongue or her urges? To be fair, it had been a few years since she'd done anything scandalous with a man, but that was no excuse.

I am such a failure... or a wanton.

"You are quite refreshing, Miss Pickwick, I'll give you that." His chuckle tickled through her chest, but it was the desire in his eyes as he gazed at her that set her ablaze again. "There will be other times."

Did that mean he wanted another intimate session between them? How intriguing.

"That being said, my first reason here is my appointment as your translator." Remembering the Egyptian book, she retrieved it then gently placed it on one of the small occasional tables. "I'll stay on for as long as the job takes, and hopefully by the end, you'll prove satisfied with my discoveries."

"Fair enough." He nodded then pushed off the shelf. "Shall

we say every day except Sundays? To start around one o'clock?"

"That would be lovely and gives me the opportunity to take breakfast with my father in the mornings as well as work around my times at the lending library."

"Yes, of course. Did you wish to start today or tomorrow?"

"I will do a bit today, but I'm afraid my mind isn't truly on my work." Heat went into her cheeks merely to hint at what they'd gotten up to.

"Understandable." He couldn't quite hide his grin. "As for my expectations, well I don't know how long a translation of a whole book should take, so I leave that up to your expertise."

She snorted. "I don't know how much of an expert I am. If I'm stumped at a passage here and there, I might need to consult my father or someone else."

"Only your father. I don't wish to tip my hand with this book should I decide to offer it at auction."

"Agreed." As the last residual trembles from the release subsided, she stifled a sigh. "Where shall I set up?"

"Oh, uh, you can make use of the library, of course, or if you require a proper desk, my study is across the hall on this level. Feel free to move there."

"Won't you have use of it?"

"Not during the hours you'll be in residence. Besides, I am working on finishing bits and bobs of renovation to the townhouse just now, so I'll be in and out. Don't wish to disturb your concentration."

Ah, so that was why he had the callouses. "Very well. Thank you, Your Grace, er, Barrington." Such a lovely and majestic name.

"It is my pleasure, for you will do much of the work. I'm afraid I'm a bit of a dunce when it comes to reading hieroglyphics or Hieratic."

"I can teach you," she managed to blurt, a second ahead of her brain.

"I might pop in between bouts of renovations." He tugged a

watch from his waistcoat pocket. "Speaking of, I need to scoot. Ring for tea or anything else you should need, and if you have a question, I'll be primarily in the drawing room, but any of the servants can fetch me for you."

She nodded and then took another glance around the library. "For the moment, I'll start my work here, but I can't promise I'll stay in the library for the duration, for I'll probably need to work close to a candle."

"You have *cart blanche* while here… Catherine." Then he was gone in the next second, while she stared at the spot he'd just vacated.

Odd, but she rather liked the sound of her name from his lips.

CHAPTER FIVE

December 19, 1816

BARR WOKE LATE that morning, and only because his valet eventually woke him at half past ten. Even still, vestiges of exhaustion clung to him as well as his mind.

After relieving himself and conducting morning ablutions, he submitted to Travers' ministrations for the toilette of the day while drinking his customary cup of strong coffee.

"The butler mentioned that you had in a lady yesterday to translate that book you found in the attics," Travers said in a conversational tone. "Will she be able to help?"

"That remains to be seen; she has barely started, and from what I understand, it could prove an involved process. She didn't have all the reference books she needed with her yesterday since she merely wished to study the book." Above everything, Barr strove to ignore the heat sneaking up the back of his neck and in his chest, for he and Miss Pickwick had done far more than studying a book yesterday.

"I assume she will return today?" The valet handed him a pair of buff-colored breeches.

"Yes, around one o'clock." He avoided meeting Travers' gaze while fussing with the breeches. "It should be interesting what we discover as she goes through the text."

"Indeed." Without further comment, the valet held out a fine lawn shirt. When Barr snatched it from his hand and began the task of tugging it over his head and then smoothing it over his torso, the wretched man spoke again. "One of the maids passing in the corridor said she heard whispers and excitable sounds coming from the room, but when she peeked inside, there was no one there."

"That *is* quite odd." Taking refuge in his coffee, Barr again refused to meet his friend's gaze. Damn, he should have closed the library door yesterday, but everything had happened so fast and had gotten out of control so quickly, he'd not thought about it. Thank goodness for the high back of the sofa that had hidden them both from view, though. "Perhaps the townhouse is haunted."

"Suddenly haunted? After all this time of living here?" Clearly, his valet wasn't convinced. He held up a waistcoat of dark green satin.

"Who can say?" After he finished the contents of his cup, Barr set it on a nearby table then allowed Travers to fit the waistcoat to his torso, huffing when the laces were slightly tightened.

"Would you like to hear my theory?"

God, no.

But he said, "Does it matter? You'll tell me anyway." And he could almost wager what he would say.

Unfortunately, Travers dragged out the anticipation by fitting Barr with the cuffs and collar then fussed with his cravat, twisting and manipulating the length of silk into the particular knot he wanted. Then and only then did the other man speak.

"I think that after you met Miss Pickwick, who is quite a handsome woman and from all accounts, intelligent, an intense connection has formed between you. When she was supposed to be studying the ancient book, you lost your damned mind by using that opportunity to study *her* body. And those sounds were utterances of her pleasure." When the valet leveled a knowing look onto Barr's face, heat again sneaked up the back of his neck. "Is my guess remotely true?"

Bloody, bloody hell.

"This is what happens when my staff have been with me for years and know me far too well," he groused but couldn't help but offer a slight grin.

"Then my hunch is correct?"

"Yes." After all, what else was there to say?

Travers' eyes widened. "I thought you might prove repressed in that regard, but the first day you have a woman into your home, hired out to translate a book for you?" He shook his head. "You lose your bloody mind and claim her right there in your library?"

"Do shut up." Apparently, he would burn to death today. "It wasn't planned. Just happened. I don't know how or why. And also, I didn't couple with her. I just, uh..." Barr tugged at his newly tied cravat knot. "I, um, brought her to release with my fingers."

The valet hooted with laughter. "Someone was desperate, and I'll wager it wasn't her."

"Yes, well..." Yet Barr couldn't help his grin. "What's done is done, but it can't happen again."

"What a bummer. Did you fuck her?"

"No, of course not. That bit of insanity was enough." But Catherine had been *quite* responsive. Even remembering it now made him semi-hard.

"Then it's not over and it will happen again."

"You can't know that."

"I know you're a man." Travers shrugged. "Whatever is between you will continue to snap and crackle until the deed is done." When Barr didn't answer, the valet went on, "What will you do now?"

"Act with decorum, of course. I've hired her to translate the book, not attend to my random, physical urges." Truly, what had happened yesterday had been an aberration and couldn't occur again.

"And while she's ensconced in your library doing just that? Where will you be?"

"That is difficult to say." Slowly, Barr slipped his arms into the rust-colored jacket Travers held out for him. "Work on the renovations."

"Coward."

He frowned. "What?"

"Instead, you could ask her to spend time with you beyond the renovations and translations during the holiday season. She can help decorate a few rooms."

"I don't know if she would be interested."

"That is why you use your manners and your charm to ask, Your Grace." Travers shook his head. "You aren't a novice at this."

"Ha. In her company, I suddenly feel that way." For far too long he had been out of practice in such things.

"Then stop thinking. Do what feels right or natural—without hiding—and see what happens." The valet nodded with encouragement. "Events in London during this time of year are sparse, most people are in the country, the weather is dreary, but the fires are lovely, and my wife has promised to do her best with meals should you wish to invite Miss Pickwick to dinner. To say nothing of taking her out to gather greenery should the weather actually break."

Oh, God.

Things were moving far too fast, and he'd acted like a sex-deprived arse yesterday, despite her being willing. Yet Travers expected an answer. After clearing his throat, Barr nodded. "I will be sure to ask her at least one of the days."

The valet's grin widened. "Do you promise?"

"Why do you care?"

"Just this. You've been a friend to me for years. I remember how happy you were with Her Grace and how devastated you were when she died." A sigh escaped Travers' throat. "You deserve to be happy again."

For long moments, Barr frowned as he thought over the words. "But—"

"Look, I'm not asking that you wed the woman. Simply enjoy her companionship, and if interesting *things* occur between you, where is the harm? It's Christmastide. Men shouldn't be alone."

Damn. He couldn't fault the valet for his advice. "I'll take your words into account. Meanwhile, instead of this jacket, I'd like the gray tweed today…"

THREE HOURS INTO Catherine's stint into working on the translation, there was finally a break in the rain. Barr had kept himself occupied in the drawing room, finishing the renovation, then he'd spent an hour re-papering the downstairs parlor, doing as much of that room as he could before he realized he didn't wish to remain a hostage to the foul weather.

By the time he returned to the library, she was enjoying tea, and suddenly he found himself famished.

"Ah, if you are quite finished hiding, you are more than welcome to join me," Cate said, as her eyes lit, and she greeted him with a soft smile.

"As much as I would like that, I wondered instead if you'd like to go on a drive since it's not raining."

"Oh!" Surprise jumped into her expression. "Why? I'm supposed to be working on this translation." She gestured with her free hand to the book that sat open with a notebook on the other side of the table from the tea service.

"Fair enough." He shrugged as if it didn't matter. "I thought you might wish to get out. Obviously, everything will be too damp and wet for walking, but going on a drive might chase away any restlessness we might have."

For long moments, she watched him from over the rim of her teacup as she took a few sips. Then she nodded. "Very well. I could stand to rest my eyes, in any event. Some of the words in the book are difficult to discern due to ink smears or fading or water damage."

"I can just imagine, but I'm glad to give you an excuse." Knots formed in his belly. Why the hell was he so nervous? It wasn't as if he were a green boy.

So ridiculous.

A half hour later saw them in his closed carriage and well underway, but the streets of May were crowded, for it seemed other people had the same idea to make the best use of an afternoon without the rain.

Barr didn't mind, for they chatted about favorite places in Mayfair and London, as well as favorite exhibits at the British Museum.

"Oh, that's a difficult question. There are far too many exhibits there I like, and for different reasons. I adore that place." Cate's eyes twinkled and he vowed he would take her there soon, to break up the monotony of translation.

"One of my favorite galleries is the Egyptian one as well as the Roman one."

She nodded. "My father enjoys that too. He often visits. One of his goals in life is to have something to donate for said exhibit."

"I hope he does, for I look forward to viewing it."

The time passed easily, for conversing with her was interesting and compelling with no awkward silences. At some point while stuck in traffic near Hyde Park, awareness shivered over him from the way she looked at him across the narrow aisle.

"Why do you stare at me like that?"

"Like what?" She was quite a cheeky woman.

"As if you wish to gobble me up." Was that crossing a line to say?

"Hmm." Cate shrugged and then winked as she removed her bonnet and gloves. "Perhaps I do, and I should treat you to the same as you did me yesterday, hmm? It's only polite."

"What?"

Before he could form some sort of protest, she kneeled before him, easily inserting herself between his splayed knees, sliding her hands up his thighs. "Has anyone ever told you that your cologne is quite intoxicating?"

"Oh?" Electric sensation twisted up his spine and through his gut at her touch. "I wasn't certain of it, but I wanted something different than what I wore when my wife was alive. It proved the first step in moving forward, though I fear it's still at a glacial pace." Yet he was thrilled she'd noticed.

"It's quite delicious, and smells like a crisp winter's morn. Reminds me of the times when my parents and I used to go into the country to visit Mama's side of the family. There were evergreens all over the property, and I remember they had holly bushes in the hedgerows. Those berries were always so pretty against the snow."

To distract himself from her proximity, he nodded. "You'll have to tell me about her at some point, if you wish." Barr could hardly concentrate on forming words since she had decided to manipulate the buttons at his front falls.

Would he let her?

"I would be happy to, but just now, I am going to assuage my curiosity about you."

His rapidly hardening length tumbled into her hands, and from the way she sucked in a breath, one would think he was quite the gift. With each moment, every breath, blood rushed into his member, further rendering it erect. "Leave off, Cate. This isn't necessary." Yet he didn't move, so apparently, he'd answered his own question.

Yes, yes, he would let her do anything she wanted to him.

"Perhaps not." Her eyes glimmered in the gloom of the over-cast late afternoon skies. "But I wish to do it anyway, for your pleasure and mine. Turnabout and all that, and I enjoy making men squirm in this way." The grin she shot him nearly saw him undone. "Let's see your mettle, hmm, Barrington?" With a grin, she manipulated the buttons of his front falls.

"Ah, Cate, how wicked you've become since meeting me."

"Don't flatter yourself. I've always had this tendency, but

when I met you, it was as if a match dropped to dry tinder."

"Well, that does kill the ego a bit, but I can't complain." A chuckle left his throat. As his semi-aroused member popped from his trousers, he spread his legs. "But you are aware the driver might hear—"

"None of that, Your Grace. The threat of discovery will only enhance such an endeavor." She caressed her fingers up and down the inside of his splayed thighs, leaving a rush of heat on his skin. "Let the possibility of discovery add an edge to our play." If they were found out, there would be hell to pay, but the race of his pulse in his ears and the throb of pure heat through his member that encouraged it to further harden fed into his curiosity.

"Do I have a choice?" The inquiry was a tad breathless, for she'd begun to caress the underside of his shaft.

"You do not. Consider it payment for what you did to me yesterday." She sent him a daring wink before she settled into her task.

The more she handled his equipage, the tighter and longer his length grew. Dear God, he wouldn't last at this rate, so he employed all the willpower he possessed into not spending prematurely. Cate curled her fingers around him; his girth fit far too well into her palm. As she experimented with various degrees of pressure, moans escaped him. With a faint grin of apparent satisfaction, she fondled his stones, squeezing and releasing, finding a rhythm she liked that incorporated both them and his length.

And it quickly worked to separate him from his sanity. "If you were a cat, I'd swear you'd be purring." His chuckle was forced, for he was drowning in sensation.

She snorted. "Mmm, does that mean I should climb into your lap?" As images of her straddling his lap flashed into his mind, she held his gaze and licked the wide head of his member. Barr hissed in a breath.

"Cate..."

"Now who is desperate?" With a laugh, she took his length into her mouth. One of his hands that rested on the leather bench curled into a fist and then relaxed when she eased off. As she bobbed up and down on his member, a faint flush stained her cheeks, and he rather thought he might form an addiction to her.

As she apparently grew more comfortable in her task, she swirled her tongue around the underside of his head and added caresses and squeezes while she worked him over with her mouth. His moans came more quickly. Eventually, he couldn't stand it any longer, so he put a hand to her head and slowly thrust, which sent his shaft deeper until the tip hit the back of her throat. She paused, and he could almost see her mind working. Would she like the sensation?

Then, she swallowed. The massaging sensation of her throat muscles on his sensitive flesh was indiscernible. "Good God," he breathed, and his finger furrowed into her hair as he framed the back of her head. "Who schooled you in that?"

She chuckled as he backed off, but she didn't decrease her rhythm. "My last lover was quite progressive in what he wanted and liked. He taught me much."

"Well, now I am reaping the rewards of those lessons." Yet jealousy stabbed through his chest for that unknown man. The more he concentrated on what she did to him, the more pleasure swam through his veins. "I am not going to last."

She squeezed his stones. "I'm counting on it," she whispered, and then contented herself with sucking on the head of his member.

"Damn," he breathed, and his hand on her head tightened, guiding her. "You are... This is... Ah!" His eyes rolled back into his head for this was quite near heaven.

"What's wrong, Your Grace?" she crooned as she worked. "You are so anxious."

Oh, but he was close to the edge. Even now, his length twitched and jerked from her handling. Pre-ejaculation seeped from his tip, and she licked it away. Cate eased her fingers beneath his stones to massage the thin skin directly behind them.

"Shit!" The word was propelled from his throat, and he couldn't recall it back before his driver heard. Would he, even now, wonder what was happening inside the carriage? He bucked his hips, sending his shaft deep, while his fingers delved into her hair.

And still Cate continued her quest to make him fall over the edge. Again and again, she twisted her fingers about his length while sucking and then soothing with her tongue, followed by taking him deeper into her mouth. Every few seconds, she would massage that highly sensitive skin behind his stones until the whole thing felt like an erotic game.

"Oh, God, do that!" Then he was gone. He lost control, and with a muffled shout, he hit release. His length pulsed as it emptied its seed into her mouth. She swallowed a few times in succession. The sight of her drinking from him was the most sensual thing, and the smugness in her expression told him she didn't mind. It only enhanced the troubling connection already between them.

Once he finished, he collapsed against the bench's back. His breath shuddered from his lungs, ragged and rapid in the silence.

"Can I trust you enjoyed yourself?" she whispered with glimmering eyes.

"So much," he whispered as he drew his handkerchief from a jacket pocket and handed it to her. "You have reminded me I'm not as old as I think."

"Ah, good." Cate wiped the lingering moisture from her cheeks and mouth. "That always serves as a lovely distraction."

"Distraction? Woman, you nearly killed me." Had relations with his wife been that intense? Perhaps at the beginning, but then they'd had children, and between that, duties to the title, parliament, and social obligations, such things had been shoved into the background. That didn't mean either way was wrong; they were merely different.

"Ha! Then you know I did it right." Calmly, she wiped her

mouth on the handkerchief, but her eyes twinkled with amusement and satisfaction. While he righted his clothing, she resumed her seat on the bench opposite with the same enigmatic smile she'd started the drive with. "You were correct. This outing has done me a world of good."

This was beyond anything he could have ever imagined, and it was quite bizarre to be indulging on anything of the sort, but as Travers had told him numerous times, life was short. But there was one burning question in his mind. "Well?" He couldn't help but ask. "Did that assuage your curiosity about that certain part of me?"

"Oh, *quite.*" Then she tucked the handkerchief into her reticule, put the bonnet on her head, and tied the ribbons. "It's a week until Christmas. Do you have plans I should account for?" Her tone was far too conversational, as if she hadn't just sucked him off so well that he'd sworn he'd seen the stars.

"Uh, no plans. As I've said, my children are away due to the weather, but I thought of decorating a few rooms for the holiday. It will serve as a break from the transition and renovation duties we're each doing."

One of her eyebrows rose. "You'll celebrate alone?"

Barr shrugged. The residual heat and shudders had faded. "I suppose, unless you would be interested?" Did he truly wish to invite her to spend more time with him? Not that they hadn't already been scandalous and shared intimacy with each other.

"I might be, indeed. Papa is involved with his paper, and I doubt he'll be aware of what time of year it is."

"You and he can join me for Christmas dinner if you'd like."

"That would be lovely. I'll tell him about those plans, but if you would like to have me postpone the translation until after the new year?"

"What?" A bit of panic rose in his chest, for the past two days had been thrilling and had given him a bit of purpose back. "No, of course not. Please continue working on the text. We don't stand on ceremony or tradition at my home."

When she nodded, she gave him a smile that had renewed interest stirring in his member. "Thank you. It's a bit lonely in the library all afternoon, or the study should I wish for a new location. Not that I expect you to wait upon my every whim."

Oh, he could find *something* to do with her to pass the time, especially after today's unexpected scandal. "I've finished the renovation in the drawing room. You can move into that room. I'd be happy to do some of my work there too. Additionally, there is the decorating to attend to." It was feeling far too domestic and that he was losing control of his previous life, but oddly, he didn't mind it as much as he'd previously assumed.

"I'm looking forward to it. Thank you. I rather think my father will hole up in his study or the Reading Room at the British Museum during these days." Oddly, there was emotion in her eyes, but they didn't well with tears. "Though I'm well versed in his eccentricities, I *have* missed some of the traditional things the holiday offers."

Perhaps it was due to the magnificent release he'd been given or the pleasant lethargy he now enjoyed, but his grin felt quite goofy. "Then I shall be happy to oblige."

What have I gotten myself into?

CHAPTER SIX

December 20, 1816

CATE COULDN'T HELP feeling quite content with her life. She'd worked the morning shift at the lending library, and now, she'd been admitted into the duke's townhouse to tackle another few hours of the translation. This time, she'd brought a couple of books her father had of Egyptian hieroglyphs to hopefully help her with figures she'd not yet seen before.

Today, she decided to work on the translation in the drawing room, where it was obvious it had been freshly papered and painted. The portions of the wall over the wainscotting had been painted a forest green while the lower portions of the wall were covered with ivory paper with pink stripes and strips of trailing green ivy vines. Aubusson rugs in matching colors covered portions of the wooden floor while heavy velvet draperies in dark green hung at the windows.

But one of the best features in the room was the sight of the duke, who sat in one of the winged-back chairs near the fireplace, where cheerful flames danced behind an ornate metal grate. The silver strands in his hair glimmered in the candlelight, for it was once more pouring rain outside.

"Good afternoon, Scarborough."

His eyes lit as he set the book he'd been reading down as he met her gaze. "Hullo, Miss Pickwick. It's good to see you again. Did you intend to work in here this afternoon?"

"I do. It's quite lovely in here, and cozy with the fire." She selected a low sofa near to his location then settled there with her books, notebook, and the Egyptian book.

"And don't forget the rain," he said with a cheeky grin. "You can't have Christmastide in England without the damned rain. Especially this year, apparently."

"You are obsessed with the weather."

He snorted. "Show me an Englishman who isn't."

Cate couldn't help but smile, for the duke was an interesting man, and he grew more fascinating as each hour went by. "There is that." She spread her books out on the table. "I've been able to make a bit of progress on the book. Luckily, it's a fairly slim volume and the writing isn't cramped though some of the symbols are vexing."

"Excellent. I look forward to helping with the translation."

She nodded. "Are you familiar with hieroglyphics?"

"A bit, but I am always willing to learn."

Mmm, did that apply to everything in life? Perhaps she would have the opportunity to discover if that was true. When she caught a bit of glitter from the corner of her eye, Cate glanced at the boxes of Christmas finery. There was even a box of freshly cut greenery.

"Did someone go out and fetch pine boughs in the rain?"

"Um, actually the footmen went out yesterday to retrieve them. I would never have anyone go out in this miserable weather, not even for pine boughs." His grin sent shivers of need down her spine. "The only thing they didn't bring back was mistletoe."

"Perhaps on the next break in the rain we could search for some."

"Excellent idea." He chuckled. "My wife was adamant the house have at least two sprigs of the plant."

"Oh, why?"

"Well, there was nothing she enjoyed more than casually drifting beneath a sprig in the hopes I would see and come over to kiss her." A bit of nostalgia crossed his face. "So she directed the footmen to hang one here in the drawing room and put another in the upstairs, private parlor."

"That is quite a sweet tradition." Cate held his gaze. "Did you humor her with kisses?"

"Of course. There was nothing like seeing her face light each time I would play into her silly scheming. My children thought it fun when they were young, but I suppose they'll never forget and perhaps will remember that whimsy is a big part of making a marriage last."

"How lovely." Was he still in love with his dead wife? Perhaps that was something she truly needed to find out. Not that there was anything between her and the duke other than desire, and it might carry over into a tryst for the length of her translation services.

"You had said previously that you enjoy the Christmastide season. Why is that?" As he spoke, Barr left his chair to settle beside her on the sofa. The heat of him seeped into her side since his shoulder brushed hers.

"Oh, my mother was quite the hostess; she adored decorating and entertaining. Every year she invited my father's colleagues for a party during this season. That always meant budging my father out of his study and making him chat with his friends as well as hers." She grinned with the remembrance. "There were parlor games and carol singing sometimes, but she had quite the knack of bringing everyone together and making everyone feel lovely."

"That certainly sounds cozy. You must miss her terribly."

"I do. Some days are worse than others." A hint of tears welled in her eyes. "This time of year is especially difficult, at times, but if I keep myself busy, the loss isn't as acute."

"Then it's even more important to keep the traditions. If you'll help with decorating, perhaps you'll feel your mother close this year."

"Thank you." She nodded. "That is kind of you."

"And I won't miss my children so much as well." Then he leaned across her to pick up the Egyptian book. Did he mean to brush his sleeve over her breasts? "How far have you gotten on the translation?"

"I'm nearing the first quarter." As an experiment, Cate slid her hand along his arm to the hand holding the book then she opened the volume to the page she'd stopped on yesterday. "If you would like to assist in the translation, I'd welcome that help." Spending time with him in any capacity was becoming difficult after what they'd shared over the past few days, for the sheer reason that she wanted more. So much tension snapped between them, so much desire and innuendo, and while she reveled in that, she needed a break from it.

It was almost as if she was becoming drunk on him or dependent like an opium addict. It was madness, and far different than what she'd shared with her previous employers turned lovers. Would he soon bed her? Oh, she hoped so. After manipulating his member yesterday in the carriage, she couldn't wait to have that appendage moving in and out of her body.

"I would be delighted to assist, but I don't know how much I'll be able to contribute."

With their heads close together and the duke holding up the book, Cate grabbed up her notebook where she'd scribbled notes and ponderances.

"Since some of the passages are faded and some are hopelessly smeared from water damage over the years, the translation has been slow and frustrating, but I can tell you what I've managed thus far." When he nodded, she continued as she consulted her book. "From what I can understand, this is the story of a son of a pharaoh."

"The one we spoke about before?"

"Not likely, but if it is, this was a son far down the line of succession because he doesn't have his own title, and it doesn't appear anything was expected of him beyond being a hunter." She shrugged. "He has apparently fallen in love with a young woman who is entirely wrong for him."

"How so?"

When she shrugged again, her shoulder brushed his, leaving heated tingles behind. "From all accounts, it seems as if this young woman is one of the slaves in the palace. The pharaoh's son knows if his father finds out, he'll order the girl's death, especially as she's not of Egyptian descent."

"Ah, bit of a shock, that." After setting his spectacles on the bridge of his nose, the duke scanned the text with his gaze. He pointed out symbols and letters he recognized. "I imagine it was difficult back then, especially if one was royalty."

"But consider the romance of it all," Cate insisted with a nod. "Sneaking about, stealing kisses when they think they're alone." She grinned. "The pair shares a mutual desire that can't be denied." When she turned to a page in the slim volume, her fingers brushed his. "One night, they met at midnight by the river. Hidden in the reeds and vegetation, they can be together, and according to the passage here, they wish to show each other the depths of their love through creative and inventive positions."

"How interesting. I suppose when one is indulging in clandestine relationships, one makes the best of them."

Cate nodded. "Then the man writes about those position as well as his love for the young woman." When she glanced at the duke, their gazes collided. "This book is a romantic documentation of his courtship of her despite the danger to them both and the forbidden words they aren't allowed to speak to each other. It's poetic prose to this woman so she might know how he feels without him saying it aloud for someone to overhear, and the pictures are a remembrance of what they've explored together."

"That is both sweet and sad."

"It is." With a frown, she turned to another page. "Especially after this passage. I managed to translate it yesterday." She tapped one of the passages. "Roughly, this line of hieroglyphs says 'though we cannot speak forbidden words of romance for fear of punishment, that doesn't diminish our truth. Love doesn't discriminate. It just is.'"

"While that is quite beautiful, it's very melancholy as well. I wonder how their story ended."

She snorted. "I think we both know the answer to that question."

"Perhaps." The duke shook himself and then left the sofa. He removed his spectacles and laid them on a small rose-inlaid table. "Perhaps we should introduce some cheer by decorating. I'll order tea and have the servants join us. It will be like having family around us."

"What a lovely idea." Slowly, Cate closed the books and then stacked everything together on the tabletop. "Are you quite close with your staff?"

Barrington shrugged. He tugged on the bellpull near the door. "I try to be. They've been with me for years, and they are loyal. I think that is more than most families can say."

"You are certainly not the sort of duke I expected." When she stood up from the sofa, she shook out her skirting. "It's refreshing."

Amusement mixed with confusion in his eyes. "What sort of duke did you think I was?" As a footman answered the summons, he quietly told the man to gather all the available servants, for they were doing an impromptu decorating party in the drawing room.

"Oh, you know type. Balding with a paunch, dissolute, full of vices, breath like garlic." When he threw her a shocked look, she couldn't help but chuckle.

Then a couple of footmen entered the room with a tall wooden ladder. Soon after, the housekeeper followed, along with the butler, and she was quickly introduced to everyone. When the footmen set work hanging a large wreath woven with red velvet ribbon over the fireplace, the cook entered the room with a rolling tea tray for everyone. Barr's valet followed.

The duke came forward. "Miss Pickwick, this is my friend and valet, Charles Travers, and his wife, Sarah. They have both been with me for more years than I can count, and Sarah is a genius in the kitchen."

"Hush, you," the cook said with a hint of a blush in her cheeks. Both she and Travers were perhaps in their early to mid-thirties, and they were adorable together. She rested her gaze on Cate. "His Grace is full of gammon sometimes, I think, but he is a decent employer, and though he is stubborn at times when we tell him he needs to put himself back out into society, I can't imagine working for anyone else."

Travers nodded. "Indeed, but he and I have been friends for more years than I can count. There is no better man in London."

"That is high praise indeed." She bestowed a smile on the valet. "I'm glad he has people like you around him."

Off to the side, Barr waved away their compliments as a hint of ruddy color rose up his neck. "I have a feeling some of this is for your benefit, Miss Pickwick."

"I doubt that. They are obviously fond of you."

The cook chuckled. "Everyone, please partake in the tea. I've brought two pots so there's enough for everyone." She included the whole company in her gaze as a few maids drifted into the room. "While we do that, perhaps we should go around the room and share one of our favorite Christmastide memories."

The whole afternoon was a gay affair as decorations went up and the assembled company related many sweet memories. There were many laughs exchanged, especially when one of the footmen related a story of how he'd fallen into a horse trough by accident on Christmas morning as a youth when he'd received a horse of his own.

While Cate indulged in her tea, she watched as the duke circulated around the room, talking and laughing with various members of the staff. He even lent a hand in placing tin bells and glass balls within greenery on the hearth. The whole thing was cozy and lovely, for the he didn't treat anyone differently. His actions tugged at her heart and were most appreciated. Being here truly felt as if she were included in a big family.

Travers drifted over to her location. "Would you like to have a tour of the house? I can show you the rooms where the duke has done renovations by himself."

"Oh! That might prove interesting." When she glanced across the room at the duke, he was occupied by directing one of the footmen hang the wreath higher over the hearth. "Are you offering the tour now?"

"Of course." There was a certain gaiety about him. He nodded at his wife, who gave him a smile in return. "It shouldn't take long."

"I welcome the break. As all of you gather together, I'm reminded of how things were when I grew up. Now, it's just me and my father. He's scatter-brained and distant when working on an academic paper as he is now. I'm not sure he even remembers it's the holiday season, even though I've mentioned it a few times."

"If he's happy, then leave him be. We all have precious little time as it is."

"Very true." As she walked with him downstairs, he told her about his history with the duke and how they'd become friends. Then they arrived at the parlor. "This is His Grace's most recent project. It hadn't been updated since he'd married the late duchess."

"It's so pretty." She peered about the space, with the crushed velvet upholstery in a pleasing rose color. Moss green accents broke up the space. One of the walls remained without paper. A wooden ladder leaned against that wall. Sheets of moss green paper stamped with thin cream and pink stripes waited on the floor. Pink draperies rested over the back of a sheet-covered sofa. "What was the color scheme before?"

"Gold and blue."

"This is far more welcoming. The duke has quite an eye for detail and color."

"He does, and what is more, he truly enjoys working with his hands even though he has the funds to pay laborers to do this in a fraction of the time." Then he led her up the stairs to the third level. "I assume you've seen the study?"

"I have. The leather chair behind the desk is quite comfortable." And said desk was massive. She wouldn't mind testing its strength if the duke wished for a tryst.

"That was the first room he renovated two years ago when his son announced his engagement." Travers showed her into a suite near the top of the stairs. "This is the duchess suite, and his next project once the parlor is finished."

Cate popped her head into the room and frowned. "It's been stripped of everything." Paper had come down, no furniture occupied the space, the floorboards had been pried up, draperies at the windows here gone, and the glass itself had shades drawn. "Why?"

"Who can say? But if I know Barrington, it was his way of closing that chapter of his life. Her Grace spent the last months of her life in this suite so she wouldn't disturb him, and for a year or so after her death, he kept the rooms locked, so this is a good step forward."

"I can understand that. Grief has no timeline, but beyond the pain, there is also healing. It seems he is making good use of walking his new path through life."

"Exactly. I'm glad for him. For too long, my wife and I were worried about him." He backed out of the suite and closed the door.

Cate nodded. "Understandable. And you aren't now?"

"Not as much. He still drags his feet about going into society, but that will come, I'll wager."

"Well, he's made impressive strides." As they went back to the second floor, where he showed her the improvements done to the dining room, she asked, "Is Scarborough interested in marrying again?"

"Marriage? I'm not certain." Travers tossed her a glance brimming with speculation. "It would depend on the woman, but I believe he needs someone in his life to keep him from hiding.

It's far too easy for him to lose himself in these projects or in collecting first editions."

"In that way, he is much like my father, I fear. Once my mother died, he buried himself in his work, even more than he had before." To that end, what *did* Barrington want from life, from her? A tryst only? Did it matter since she was enjoying their mutual carnal play? Life was short, indeed, so why was she questioning herself if she found enjoyment and delight in what she'd shared with the duke already? Deciding none of it mattered, she thanked the valet for the tour as they paused at the doors to the drawing room.

"About that Egyptian book His Grace has found?"

"Yes?"

The valet frowned. "Encourage Scarborough to sell it quickly."

"Why? It's quite a find."

"Agreed, but things like that should have stayed buried. Now that you both have opened it and are now translating it, you'll probably end up cursed."

"What?" Cate snorted with amusement. "It's an erotic storybook that has mentioned nothing about a curse."

"Who can say?" Travers shrugged. "The Ancient Egyptians were a clever lot, weren't they? We will never know how such things work."

"True, but I promise to be careful." Then she entered the drawing room and flashed a smile when the duke glanced at her with questions in his eyes.

Over the course of the next hour, the room was splendidly decorated and once finished, there was no denying the holiday season was well underway. Eventually, the gathering broke up and she was only too happy to give her thanks to the staff.

Once alone with the duke, Cate smiled. "This has been one of the loveliest days I've passed in quite some time, but I should probably go home. Papa will want his dinner in a couple of hours, and I need to continue work on the translation."

"Nonsense. It's barely four o'clock. Your father probably doesn't take the evening meal until seven, and besides, from what you've told me about him, he's no doubt at the Reading Room in the British Museum."

There was that. "Yes, but the translation—"

"It can wait. After all, that young couple in love has been dead for centuries. Their story can remain a secret for a few days." He winked. "I have some impressive first editions tucked away in the library if you'd like to see them."

"So Travers mentioned, and yes, I would be delighted." Perhaps she could encourage a kiss from him as well.

"Excellent, and since there are a few decorations remaining, you can tell me where to place them in that room."

"Yes, let us see what we can get up to in the library. Anything is possible surrounded by books, hmm?" It would seem this day would just keep getting better.

CHAPTER SEVEN

B ARR COULDN'T BELIEVE his luck, for he'd managed to extend his time with Cate before she left for the day. Oddly, he looked forward to her company each day.

God, Travers is going to tease me mercilessly.

Shoving that thought from his mind, he closed and locked the door, then laid the box of decorations on a small table near a leather chair. "Since my wife died, I've found collecting and selling rare books has kept my mind occupied. At times, I'll be lost in one of the books."

"And then you'll decide you simply can't bear to part with it?" she asked as she swept the shelves with her gaze.

"Exactly. There is so much knowledge in the world, and it's a tempting prospect to tiptoe through all of it without being distracted."

"I can understand that." She turned about. "Where are your first editions?"

"Just there." Barr pointed to the shelf at the far end of the room where the candlelight didn't quite penetrate. "On the top shelf. That is why the ladder is there. Wheel it over to where you want it and go ahead and make the climb."

"Truly?" The excitement in her eyes matched her tone.

"Of course. I don't gatekeep my treasures." As he spoke, he drifted closer to the ladder. "If you're afraid of heights, I'll go up."

"No, no. I was taken aback that you don't keep them under lock and key." Then she hitched up her navy skirting and mounted the first rung of the ladder.

"There is no need. I rarely leave the house, and most I don't keep under this roof for long. A few times each year, I attend auctions for rare books and valuable jewelry and the like." Did he peek up her skirts as she climbed to reach the top shelf? Yes, yes he did, for as Travers was keen to remind him, he wasn't dead yet. "It amuses me to see how much people will bid on a book that's labeled as rare or first edition. Most people don't care what the subject matter is. They just want bragging rights."

"That's what my father says about his colleagues." When she lifted onto her toes and stretched for the book she wanted, he stood at the bottom of the ladder with his heart in his throat for fear she'd fall. "Oh, good heavens, some of these are marvelous!"

It made him inordinately pleased that she liked his collection. "I think so as well. There are some volumes of Shakespeare, Keats, a bit of everything, really. Even treatises on farming, agriculture, etiquette, and other subjects."

"You even have books from around the world." Awe threaded through her voice. "My stars, there is a book of Arabian fairytales!"

He grinned up at her. "Is that something you are interested in?"

"Oh, yes! I adore the stories from far-flung lands. They are so interesting to study, and much different from what we've known here." She caressed the spines with her fingertips with a lover's touch. "My father would love to see this collection."

High praise, indeed. "He is welcome anytime, though if what you've said of him is true, I might have a difficult time in evicting him."

A snort of laughter issued from her. "That is very true." After browsing for a few moments, she came down the ladder. At the bottom, she turned about and looked at him with desire in her eyes that matched what was pushing through his veins. "There is something about a library that makes me feel… everything. Don't you agree?"

How the hell was he lost already, and he hadn't yet touched her today? But he nodded and said, "Absolutely." Then he slipped a hand behind her nape, dragged her roughly to him, and kissed her as if he couldn't have enough.

Perhaps he couldn't, for it was much like a match dropping to dry tinder.

It appeared Cate felt the same, for she kissed him back with the same ardor, and when he trapped her between his body and the ladder, she didn't offer resistance. As if he were a bee and she had the last bit of honey, Barr slid his palms down her sides and then back up again to cup her breasts through the fabric of her dress. "Far too many barriers," he murmured at her lips then eased them along the side of her neck. The soft skin there drew him onward until he nuzzled the crook of her shoulder while the faint floral scent of her further worked to see him undone.

Eventually, she lifted her arms in order to clutch at the ladder. Her eyes opened and she peered at him with passion-drugged depths, her kiss-swollen lips slightly parted. "Are you a decent man or an indecent man, Barrington?" She cocked a light brown eyebrow, and it nearly sent him over the edge.

"Which do you want me to be?" Damn, he was reckless, at least around her, and what was more, he no longer cared. There was a certain freedom found in giving in to this wicked, scandalous side where he didn't need to be so careful.

"Right now? I don't want decent." She winked and then moistened her lips. "Think you can manage that?"

How much did he adore this strong-willed side of her? "Let's find out." With a bit of a growl, Barr curled his fingers into the bodice of her dress, and with a couple of determined yanks, he had the fabric of the garment down as well as the underclothes, until her breasts were bared to his hungry gaze. When she gasped, he couldn't help his grin, for those modest charms were only part of what drew him to her.

The look in her eyes dared him to pleasure her, but when she smiled, used one of her hands to reel him closer with his cravat, that was all the permission he needed.

Once more, he kissed her, took full possession of her lips as he bedeviled her nipples into hard peaks. As soft sounds of pleasure left Cate's throat, she squirmed on the ladder, her back arching, which put her breasts more firmly into his care.

No words were said; they didn't need any, for this form of communication was quite enough. For several moments, they shared kisses and caresses. He rolled and plucked her nipples until she writhed against that ladder with her eyes closed and her cheeks flushed, the fingers of one hand gripped tight on the side of the ladder. If given the chance, he could spend an hour concentrating just on her perfect breasts, but he was already hard enough to drill through the wall, so time was of the essence, and this time, he wanted to fully claim her body.

"Barr, I… ooh…"

"Is that what a decent man would do?"

"Well, it *is* rather basic." Yet her words held a breathless quality.

"Hmm." He brushed the pads of his thumbs over her nipples and grinned when a shiver racked her shoulders. "I'll need to try harder." Then, dipping his head, he licked one of those lovely buds, before taking it into his mouth.

"Oh, I… Ah…" When she slipped on the ladder, he moved her firmly back onto it, so her arse rested on one of the treads.

"None of that. I'm not done with you yet." Barr explored the bits of her body not covered by clothing with his fingers, his tongue, and his lips. Could he bring her to release without spending in his breeches? Did he have enough control? They were about to find out. Putting all thought to his own comfort to the back of his mind, he shoved a hand beneath her skirting to caress the inside of her thighs, urged them as far apart as they could comfortably go. "I rather think it's your turn to be driven insane." And he dropped to his knees in front of her.

"Dear God." Her eyes rounded and she shook her head. "That's not necessary, but…" Those creamy thighs quivered. Anticipation reflected in her gorgeous eyes. "Surely you cannot mean to…"

"Oh, but I do, and I will." He winked. "My wife didn't much enjoy this particular act, but I'll wager you welcome it when a man does wicked things like this, hmm?" Looking his fill at her private bits, he then flicked his gaze to her face as he sobered for a few seconds. "Bid me nay, Cate, and I'll cease immediately." After all, this might be a line that was drawn.

Her breathing was already ragged. "I haven't cried foul yet, have I? Oh!" Her squeal of surprise when he licked that warm flesh at her center tugged a snort from him.

The act of pleasuring a woman orally was something he secretly enjoyed, but he never thought he would have much opportunity for that. From all accounts, Cate liked this type of play, for she'd rested a hand at the back of his head and urged him closer.

As he spread her open with one hand, he continued to caress the inside of her thighs with the other. Easily he found the pearl at her center, teased it with his tongue, and she shook with the beginnings of sensation. Soon, he settled on a rhythm he liked, and he repeated the cycle of teasing, suckling, and licking. The half-stifled sounds she made would drive him mad, and each one was more frantic than the last. Tiny pinpricks of pain kept him on the edge as she pulled his hair and squirmed in his hold only enhanced his own desire, and when she bucked her hips against his mouth, he grinned, hummed at her flesh for she was close.

"How is it you send me to the point of flying so soon?" Her body shook and she tossed her head.

"It's that damned connection between us, but by all means, let the wave take you." Again, he applied himself with renewed effort at that slippery button and dared to penetrate her passage with first one finger and then another as he massaged a specific part of her that should drive her to insanity. Her gasp of surprise echoed on the air. "How…?"

"You forget that I was married for over twenty years, and in the time since, I haven't been a monk." The pursuit of pleasure and learning the secrets to a woman's body gave him much the same satisfaction that collecting first editions did.

"Oh, you…"

A strangled sort of scream ripped from her throat the second he suckled hard at the nubbin, and he grinned as Cate fell into carnal bliss. Contractions tremored around his fingers, and his shaft pulsed in response. Damn, he'd never been so hard, but the discomfort was forgotten as he watched the expressions flit over her face—wonder, pleasure, amazement, exhaustion… hunger. Though he'd thought her beautiful before; now she was ethereal, angelic, transcendent in that bliss when her back arched and she squirmed while he continued to tease that tiny bundle of nerves, keeping her trapped on that ladder.

"I'll wager I'm not decent now."

"No, you are not." Near hysterical, Cate sagged against the treads. "Dear God." One hand drifted to a breast to pluck at a pink nipple, and he almost shot his wad right there. Cheeky woman that she was, she met his gaze and that eyebrow rose again. "Is that all you've got, Your Grace?"

He tugged a handkerchief from his waistcoat pocket then wiped his cheeks and chin. "Fuck, no." What was it about this woman that man him want to break every societal rule there was? Yet it was somehow freeing to be the man he always assumed he could be, do the things, speak the way he'd always wished but had been bound by responsibility and convention.

With her, there was none of that. In fact, in Cate's company, there was no expectation beyond the exchange of mutual pleasure. And it was a powerful aphrodisiac.

She pushed off the ladder to let a hand drift down his chest and abdomen until she cupped the hardened bulge at the front of his breeches. "What do you plan to do about it then?"

Now was exactly the moment he'd been waiting for. Tossing

away the handkerchief, he said, "This." Without further comment, Barr scooped her into his arms, carried her over to one of the leather sofas, laid her on it then followed her down. "We have danced about this moment long enough, so today, I mean to share more with you than just the preludes."

And he kissed her again because he could… because he had to; she'd cast her web over him far too well.

I might be in a spot of bother.

CHAPTER EIGHT

CATE WAS DROWNING in this man. There was simply no other word to describe it. She reveled in the weight of him atop her body, the hardness of him mixed with the buttery soft leather of the sofa at her back.

Wrenching at his cravat, she kissed the skin she managed to uncover, but it wasn't enough. Was it desperation that drove her to seek out more of him or was it simply passion that had swept her away? In the end, it didn't matter, for she would enjoy him any way he would give to her. Residual tremors throbbed through her core from that release he'd given her, and while it had been lovely and satisfying, she needed more from him.

So much more.

"Hold." The duke pulled away to rest on his knees between her splayed legs. His chest heaved while his dark blue eyes twinkled in the low illumination of this part of the library. "What would you say to trying out one of the carnal positions listed in the book?"

"Ha! I would be all for it, but I need to study the drawings further. I've only concentrated on the text thus far."

"I suppose we should be cautious lest we injure ourselves doing something naughty that would prove difficult to explain."

"Just that." She nodded. Then a new idea formed. "Switch places with me."

"What?"

"Exactly what I said." Tapping his hip, Cate struggled into a sitting position on the leather. "Lie on your back." Once he did so, and it was quite obvious of how aroused he was at the front of his breeches, she quickly straddled him. "Much better." Then she leaned over his chest and captured his lips with hers, kissed him with every ounce of feeling while she ground herself on him in the hopes of making him feel as crazed as she did.

While he groaned, an expression of stark need flitted across his face. "Damn it, woman, do you have any idea of what you are doing?"

"I have a fair notion." Just feeling the hard evidence of his arousal as it rubbed against her center through the layers of clothing made her mad to have him moving within her.

"Minx." The cheeky duke once more set out to pleasure her breasts by rolling her nipples from root to tip.

Wild sensation flooded her body. Surely, she wouldn't be tossed over the edge with only breast play, but it was entirely possible. "How am I such a wanton when in your company?" Perhaps she needed to lock herself away as a menace to society with this sexual appetite, but then, why was it socially acceptable for men to have such urges but it was frowned upon for women to enjoy such things?

"There are things in this world that have no explanation," he murmured between sucking and nipping her nipples or dragging his lips along the side of her neck. "You, I think, are one of them."

"Is that a bad thing?" As she spoke, Cate cupped his bulging length through the fabric of his breeches, and he hissed out a warning.

"No. God no." Need danced across his face when she freed his hot, hard shaft from his front falls. Even more so when she gave it a squeeze before sliding her curled fingers up and down that member. "Catherine, no teasing. I'll barely last as it is."

"I guess that leaves me no choice." With a mock pout, she rose up on her knees, moved her skirting out of the way, took him once more in hand, guided his tip to her opening, and then with a soft grin, she impaled herself onto his shaft, stones deep, until he'd fully penetrated her body.

And it was glorious.

Their groans blended together with the sound of the rain. The firm grip of his hands on her waist reminded her of his strength, and not for the first time did she wish they were naked, but then she rocked her hips, wriggling about to make certain he was well seated within her while he thrust upward.

Heated bliss became her world, and with every crash of them coming together, her eyes threatened to cross. The length of him filled her so gorgeously, and when she leaned over him, the base of his shaft rubbed over the swollen button at her center to leave shivering tingles behind.

"Dear heavens…" She blew out a breath as she stared down at him. "This is lovely, of course, but I want more from you, Barrington. I need you deeper, want to feel it harder." Would that make her seem desperate?

He nodded. "God, it's so refreshing to couple with a woman who knows what she wants." After another strong thrust, he encouraged her off him. "One second." Before she knew what he was about, he left the sofa and then plucked her off that piece of furniture as if she weighed nothing. Moments later, he relocated them both, hefted her upward and used the nearest bookshelf as leverage at her back. Since he was tall and well built, she felt delicate and dainty in his arms. "Perhaps this is more to your liking?" He speared into her and it was so raw and real, and he was quite a decent size, that she cried out.

"Oh, mercy, yes, that's wonderful!" Would the servants hear her exclamation? Her pulse rushed so hard through her veins it pounded in her ears. Unable to deny herself from touching him, she stroked a hand along his jaw. The faint prickle of stubble rasped against her skin. A muscle twitched beneath her fingertips. With every beat of her heart, she feared she'd shatter from need or from him moving in and out of her passage. For this one moment, she wished only to feel his lips and to have his body sliding against hers. Worrying about scandal could wait; trying to puzzle out her future would benefit from a delay. In this one fleeting second, there was only her and him—the man who'd slipped through her fingers. "Give me more."

"I never thought you would prove voracious, but damn that's attractive." He crushed his mouth to hers, claiming her lips with a strength she couldn't deny; her senses were consumed by this man. The muscled length of him pressed into her softer body while the hard shelf cut into her back, but the dratted duke pulled out of her body. His arms around her felt like iron bands, his fingers fire as he played them up and down her sides. The warmth of his tongue as he tangled it against hers sent heat between her thighs. She moaned into his mouth and burrowed closer. His clean, crisp scent wafted into her nose and left his indelible stamp upon her brain.

This man was her employer, and what they were doing together was wrong, yet she couldn't call a halt to it even if she'd wanted to. What was wrong with her that she ended up in carnal relationships with men in authority over her? Perhaps she didn't wish to open that particular box in her mind. Instead, Cate threaded her fingers through the silky hair at his nape. She stood on tiptoe to feel the full extent of his kiss. Her sensitive nipples rubbed against the front of his jacket, and she moaned from the exquisite torture.

The heat of his hands seeped into her rear as he gripped her derriere. His fingers feathered over her skin, and she shifted in order to spread her legs, locked her ankles at the small of his back, hoping he'd stroke her pulsing button.

When he drew abstract patterns over her buttocks, she wrenched away to pepper his chin with kisses. "Stop teasing. I need you inside me."

"Where is the fun in that, though?" He grasped her hips and ground his pelvis into hers, teasing her opening with his tip. "Yet things *are* quite urgent."

"Barrington!" Daring much, she drew a hand between their bodies and caressed the impressive length of him. His breath hissed. She smiled. "Don't make me stroke you off, for I will, but I'll be quite perturbed if you don't finish me."

"Such a managing baggage." The head of his member rubbed along her folds. A host of shivers fell down her spine and clashed with the ones invading her insides. "I rather adore it." He shoved into her passage without warning, and then Cate's world dissolved beneath a wave of pleasure. "Damnation, you feel good." He pulled out only to thrust again. The duke groaned and held his position, fully sheathed inside her. His breath stirred the loose hair at her temple.

There were no words she wanted to waste on how *he* made *her* feel. There was plenty of time for that at a later date. She grasped his shoulders and tilted her hips, wriggled them to take him in as far as she could. His thick, long length filled her, stretched her more than she'd ever been. Each tiny movement on his part set off a flutter of sensation through her core. Her insides tingled and tightened. She pulled him closer, wanting him to move yet hoping they could remain like this forever.

She'd never felt such a bond with anyone before. A tiny piece of her heart unexpectedly flew into his keeping. *Oh, dear, that is not good.*

Barrington held her steady with his hands beneath her thighs. His gaze softened and a mixture of awe and pleasure illuminated his expression. He closed his eyes and moved within her. Each penetration sent glorious sensations through her body.

With each slow, gentle thrust, Cate lost her grip on reality. "This is lovely, but... I want wild, Your Grace. I want you, uninhibited." Was that really her voice that sounded far too graveled and smoky?

He grunted. "Fuck. I don't want our joining to be *lovely*."

"Then do something about it." A tired smile curved her kissable lips. "You are guiding this seduction."

"Ha. I rather think that is a lie." But his rhythm increased as did his bid to claim her. Stronger. Harder. Faster. Each slide sent her closer to the edge.

"Barrington, send me flying." Desperation filled her voice. Cate dug her fingernails into his shoulders.

"I'm trying." He pumped into her. Each thrust sent intense sensation racing along her spine.

It was rather lovely to let go of her control and in doing that, the relaxation found within the act somehow enhanced the feelings unexpectedly brought into it. To say nothing of his impressive stamina. Cate whispered encouragement as she clawed at his shoulders and met his final drive. Over and over, he went. Deeper he drove until she was completely lost in him and what he was doing. In an odd part of her brain, she wondered if the Egyptians in that book ever coupled against a wall and if they did, was it in the palace? A few books tumbled to the floor around them.

"Tell me you're close." Need graveled his voice as he pounded into her and his fingers dug into her thighs.

"I can be." As he watched with hunger shadowing his eyes, she put a hand between their bodies and worked her own button. "Oh, goodness." The faster she rubbed that nubbin, the more the back of her hand brushed the root of his member. It seemed to inflame him, for his thrusts grew frantic and uninhibited. "Barr!" Release came over her quickly, and intense, and she gasped from it.

But he kept going, and when she went over again, she truly thought she might expire, for her body shuddered, threatened to break apart, and a half-stifled scream escaped her throat.

Seconds later, he followed her into the void, grinding into her as his length pulsed. Her inner walls squeezed around him in a series of frantic flutters. His member shuddered and pulsed. With a stifled shout, he thrust once more, but they were both spent.

As his ragged breathing echoed in her ears, he eased her down his body, and once she found her footing, she melted into him. Her skirts fell into place, but she swayed. He bundled her into his arms, and she sighed at the luxury of everything that had happened. One of her favorite things after intercourse was being held by a man to bask in that residual feeling of bliss.

When she stirred, he kissed the top of her head and then released her. She offered him a tired smile. "You were correct, Your Grace. That was *more* than lovely." She cupped his cheek then went further to furrow her fingers into his hair at his nape simply to extend the intimacy. "And better than I could imagine, especially after all that teasing."

"Damnation, that was unexpected," he said as he leaned into her, keeping her pressed between him and the books. "God, you were amazing." Such honesty threaded through his voice that she warmed from the praise.

"So were you. I'm impressed, Scarborough." For a bit, she was content to be held because she adored how a man's strength felt around her, and he was quite accommodating as they came back from the heights.

Eventually, he pulled away to tuck himself back into his breeches and right his clothing. "I suppose this means everything has changed."

"Only if you wish it." Cate frowned as she tugged her bodice back into place. Surely, he wouldn't demand marriage merely because they'd given into passion. "I should return to the translation."

"No." The duke shook his head. "Let's order tea and have a chat. After the things we've gotten up to, I'd like to know you a bit better. I don't want the heat to be all there is between us."

Well, that was quite unexpected, and it sent knots of worry into her belly. "Why?"

He shrugged as his expression turned enigmatic. "Translation work is long and exhausting, and it's the Christmastide season besides." Once he moved across the room, he unlocked the door and pulled it open. "I don't want you to think I only value your presence to relieve tension or for a bit of slap and tickle." Then he yanked on a brocade bell pull. "I hold more respect for you than that."

"Oh." That was exceedingly different from her previous two trysts with employers. "That would be quite interesting. Thank you." What did that mean going forward? She couldn't begin to say, but *something* had shifted between them during that coupling, and it both gave her a bit of hope as well as discomfited her. "Did you wish to move back into the drawing room?"

"No, this will do nicely." He pointed to the box he'd brought with him. "I thought we could do a bit of decorating in here, merely to mark the passing of the season."

She nodded. "All right." With a queer little tremor around her heart, she cleared her throat. "Allow me a few moments to refresh myself then I'll be happy to join you."

"As luck would have it, I have just two months ago installed a water closet at the end of the corridor on this level." With a wink, he ushered her into the hallway. "With a flush toilet. It was insanely expensive, but I figured if I were doing renovations, I wanted to modernize in every way I could. That was one of them."

"How interesting. Thank you." As she made her way along the corridor, she tried to wrap her head around the man the duke truly was, and why she was running a huge personal risk being with him in such a way, for sooner or later, she feared she would do something silly or stupid, like give away her heart.

And that had ended horribly the last time.

CHAPTER NINE

BARR ACCEPTED A cup of tea from Cate, and when their fingers brushed, heat tingled up to his elbow and interest shivered into his shaft. How could he want her again so soon after what they'd just done as well as his age? But there it was, unable to be ignored.

He nodded his thanks and gladly took a sip of the hot beverage while his mind spun. *I fucked the woman I hired to translate a book.* What the hell was wrong with him? Dukes didn't act as if they were six deprived degenerates, and especially not after a few days within meeting a new woman. Perhaps he needed to call for his physician. Surely, there must be something wrong with him.

Suddenly, the silence became deafening. "Tell me about your hopes for the future. Do you have dreams you wish to meet?"

"Oh." Cate's eyebrows rose with surprise. That same emotion reflected in her eyes. "To be honest, I haven't thought that far ahead. What with working at the lending library and then helping Papa with his research, I find myself lost quite a bit during the year." She tapped a fingernail against the side of her porcelain cup. "If I have the chance, I would like to travel. It doesn't matter where; I just need somewhere to start. But ideally, I'd adore visiting the places I've read about around the world that I come across in research."

"Now that my children are grown and having their own lives,

80

I, too, would like to travel. Especially after spending years collecting and then selling first editions." At least they had that in common. "In fact, I've long thought that sponsoring a dig in Egypt would be fascinating work. Can you imagine what we could find beneath the sands of time?"

"It's incredible to think about," she said with shining eyes at the possibility. "My father has a colleague who has discovered a Roman pavement on his country estate. It's made Papa mad with jealousy, but finds like that are popping up everywhere. It's as if the world is hovering on the edge of another Great Enlightenment." She set her cup into its saucer then laid them both on the low table in front of her. "With each find, the possibility of history changing is upon us, and that can only be good as we work to understand the world better."

In his mind's eye, he saw himself working alongside Cate in a far-flung, sunny locale as they pored over pottery shards and ancient scrolls. Was that the future he wanted? At the moment, he couldn't say.

"When you think about the travel aspect, would you do that as a married woman?" It was bad form of him to ask, but he burned with curiosity.

"I suppose if I met a man I rubbed on well enough with, and if he were to ask for my hand, I might marry." When she shrugged, she gave him a rueful grin. "Of course, that would assume I'd fall in love with a man who had a bit of coin to his name."

There was no expectation in her eyes and no hint in her voice, which was remarkable after what they'd just shared not a half hour past.

"That would help things along, hmm?" Once he drained the contents of his teacup, she offered to refresh it, and he gladly accepted.

As she poured out, Cate asked, "What of you? Where do you see your future going since your children are grown and one is already married? Will you keep yourself to this townhouse and wait about until you can bounce a grandchild on your knee?"

"Ha!" While he thought over his answer, Barr put another couple of seed cakes onto his plate. "I'm not certain if my son and his wife wish to have children right away, but only time will tell. As for me, I mean to continue my renovations."

"While that is well and good, they won't last forever. What will you do after that?"

He shrugged. "Start in on repairs to Scarborough Hall?" Then he couldn't help but laugh. "In all seriousness, some of those have already been set into motion, especially since my mother resides there and I want to make her last years easier."

"Will you move out there permanently?"

"Oh, I think not. While I adore the wildness of Cornwall and being so close to the sea, London has my heart, and I need to remain close due to parliament and my causes, but should the weather clear next summer, I'd like to make the journey."

"I'm sure your son will be happy to see you." She nibbled on a jam tart. When a dollop of blackberry jam stuck to the corner of her mouth, he knew a mad urge to kiss it away, but she caught it with the tip of her tongue, and he could breathe again. "Do you think you'll marry again, perhaps have a second family?"

Another difficult question to answer. Barr heaved out a sigh. "I don't know. While I'll admit, the lure of having the companionship of a second wife is strong, I am not certain I would want children at this stage of my life. If I indeed wished to travel, I wouldn't want to put my pregnant wife or young children through the rigors of such."

"That's understandable."

He nodded, watched her finish off the jam tart. "Do *you* want children?"

"Oh, heavens." A tinkling sort of laughter escaped her. "At my advanced age? I'm not certain that is even possible."

For a woman of her age, she had much still to learn. "It is. My wife died in childbirth at an advanced age. Both she and the babe perished five years ago."

"Ah, I'd wondered how she died." Briefly, she touched his arm, and another few intense tingles shot up to his elbow. "I'm so sorry. That must have been a difficult time."

"It was." He nodded. "The pregnancy was unexpected because we assumed age would have prevented that."

"That is one of those things much more study and research is needed upon." With a frown, Cate shook her head. "Yet since women are often overlooked in a myriad of reasons, I don't see that happening any time soon." She took a sip of tea. "But for me personally? I don't even know if my body can achieve such a state, truth to tell. Both of my affairs didn't result in a pregnancy, even if there was a bit of a fright once."

How interesting. "But if it did? If this one does?" He hated himself for asking, but he couldn't help it. The connection between them was spilling into other aspects of his life that went far beyond the carnal.

"Oh, Barr, I don't know. It would depend on many things, I suppose, but I don't wish to talk about that right now." When her lips turned down with a frown, he wanted to do nothing more than kiss her cares and worries away. "And I don't wish to become an obligation. There is nothing flattering or welcome about that."

"Fair enough. Then let us finish tea and move on to decorating."

She nodded. "Thank you."

Yet why did the idea of calling the woman beside him his wife keep bouncing around his head all of a sudden?

DESPITE WHAT CATE had told the duke, now that the euphoria from the coupling had faded, worry came to take its place, for there had been no efforts to prevent a possible pregnancy.

While he placed a few evergreen boughs on some shelves,

she nestled tin bells and glass balls within the greenery.

If she *did* find herself increasing, no doubt the duke would offer out of obligation or a sense of duty. She didn't want a husband in that way. It seemed like cheating, and she meant what she said. She would have a husband for love or not at all. But if she *was* pregnant, she'd be shunned from society, to say nothing of losing her position at the lending library. Her father's academic aspirations would be shattered. They would have to leave London, and he would probably forfeit his professorship at Cambridge.

Was an affair worth that, even if the duke was handsome, intelligent, and quite skilled?

"Never say you are woolgathering while decorating." Amusement threaded through Barr's voice as he put a wad of red velvet ribbons into her hands.

"I apologize. There is much on my mind just now." She tied some of the bows to the greenery he'd already placed. Then she peered at a few tin soldiers he'd tucked within the branches. "These look old and quite loved."

He nodded and was a bit misty-eyed. "Those belonged to my son from when he was a boy. There was nothing more he adored for a few years than playing with his soldiers and enacting battles." With a shake of his head, he sent her a grin. "If I'm remembering correctly, he also had a few cannons, an artillery wagon, a supply wagon, as well as sets of both English and French military units. For the life of me, I have no idea what happened to most of those toys. These are the ones that remain."

"Perhaps he took them with him. It's sweet that you remember him each year with the decorations." Seeing him in a more vulnerable state than he'd been before allowed her a glimpse of another aspect of his life. "Even though he can't be here specifically, he'll be here in spirit."

"Indeed. I didn't realize how much I would miss them during this time of the year."

The emotion in his voice tugged at her heart. "Surely this

wretched weather won't last forever. Roads will dry out and travel will once more be accomplished with relative ease." As she spoke, Cate closed the distance between them. She laid a hand on his arm. "If you are this affected, imagine how your children are as well. This is probably one of the first times they have been away from home—either here or Cornwall—and that will mean next year, you'll have them underfoot. The reunion will be all the sweeter."

How lovely it was for him to have that in his life. Since it was just her and her father, she'd never known the feeling of being part of a large family. Of course, she wasn't truly anything to the duke other than perhaps a lover over and above his translator, so she would never have cause to meet the other members of his family, so she reminded herself not to become too curious about them.

"Only time will tell." The deep rumble of his voice tickled through her chest. "I just want them to find happiness." He rested a hand atop hers on his arm.

"Does that include yourself, Barr?" she asked in a soft voice. "Don't count yourself out on that front merely because you assume your usefulness in this life is over."

"Shall I be honest?"

"Of course." When he put a curled finger beneath her chin and tilted her head up so their gazes connected, she trembled with anticipation.

"Since finding the scandalous Egyptian book and meeting you, I have felt a renewed sense of purpose." Then he lowered his lips to hers in a sweet, gentle kiss that both scattered her thoughts and renewed her worries.

"Ah, well, that reminds me." Quickly pulling away and out of his reach, Cate moved to place the remainder of the bows. "I should concentrate fully on working through that translation. I'm sure you'd like for me to finish by Christmas."

Would she see him again socially after that?

A huff left his throat. "There is no need for haste in this. I'd like it done right, not sloppily due to the impending holiday."

She nodded. "I'll see what I can do all the same." Did that mean she wanted their affair to end prematurely? Or was she afraid that her heart might be engaged the longer she spent in his company? If it wasn't already heading in that direction. Needing a distraction, she said, "Could you please move one of the more solid chairs over here beneath this mirror?" The looking glass in question was an ornate piece set in a scrolled, gilded frame in the shape of an oval. "I'd like to hang a bow on the top. It will look so pretty when catching the light."

"Of course." Was it her imagination, or did his expression fall slightly? Once he brought over a chair with a sturdy wooden back and a rather hard cushion, he placed it beneath the mirror. "Are you sure you wish to climb that? I can hang the ribbon."

"Do stop, Scarborough. I'm not a helpless woman." But she did accept his hand as help when she hiked up her skirting and then climbed atop the chair. When she was obliged to reach over her head a bit more than she'd anticipated, she teetered, but Barr was right there, anchoring her with his hands on her hips… and she rather liked the security. "There." With a bit of fussing with the ribbon to encourage it to lay correctly, she smiled at her reflection in the mirror. "See how lovely that is?"

"I do, indeed," he said in a soft voice as he stared up at her. Then he offered his hand. "Now, come down. I don't need a potential apoplexy wondering if you'll teeter off that chair."

"Such a spoilsport," she murmured, but before she could use his assistance to climb off the piece of furniture, the mirror trembled on its hook, then as she stared, the whole piece tipped forward and came away from the wall. "Barr!"

That cry of alarm spurred the duke into action. In seconds, he whisked her off the chair and into his arms moments before the mirror fell forward. With a horrific noise, it crashed onto the chair then subsequently the floor, shattering into several pieces. Had she been still standing on the chair, it would have smacked into her and knocked her to the floor, possibly injuring her quite handily.

"Oh, goodness." Cate's heartbeat pounded out a frantic rhythm, and she wrapped her arms about the solidness of his shoulders. "If you hadn't been quick…"

He nodded as he tightened his grip ever so slightly. "You could have been rendered unconscious or worse. It's a heavy mirror but the frame is even more so." Peering into her eyes, he asked, "Are you hurt?"

"No, I'm fine. Just shaken. What an odd accident." Yet she didn't try to wriggle out of his hold. Then she gasped. "What if it wasn't an accident?"

"What the devil does that mean?" Concern shadowed the blue pools of his eyes as he carried her across the room.

"What if what your valet said is true? What if that Egyptian book is truly cursed and now that bad luck is transferring to us?" It was far-fetched, of course, but it bore mentioning.

"Truly?" He scoffed. "What poppycock."

"Is it, though?"

He frowned. "Though there have been some weird, and possibly unexplainable incidents in my family over the years."

"Such as?"

Barr gently deposited her on a sofa. "Well, two years ago, my mother nearly drowned when she made a misstep and tumbled into the Serpentine." He rubbed a hand along his jaw. "About ten years back, my father fell down the stairs, resulting in a broken arm which had to be painfully set. And when my sister was younger, she was thrown from a horse. She remained unconscious for two days after that from hitting her head on a tree." His frown was fierce. "As for me, I've had terrible luck with a particular goose in Hyde Park near the Serpentine. Every time I visit, I'm bedeviled by him."

She didn't want to laugh, but she couldn't help it as she imagined what that must look like. "You are going to need to let me witness *that* in person." Then she sobered. "No wonder your father or grandfather hid the book away."

"I rather doubt any of that is connected to a curse. There are no such things." With the shake of his head, the duke yanked on the bell pull.

"Who can say? It's an entertaining thought, but there is not enough evidence about either the book or its original provenance."

"This is true. My father certainly never mentioned the book, and if Grandfather was the one who hid it, he didn't let on that he'd traveled, but he might have bought the book from someone who did."

"Someone who might, even now, be dead," she said in a quiet voice.

"Bah." Then the butler arrived at the door. Quickly, Barr gave an explanation of what had occurred. "Please ask the housekeeper to bring in a cool cloth and perhaps tea to settle Miss Pickwick's nerves. We'll also need a maid and footman in here to tidy the mess."

"Oh, Your Grace, there is no need to make a fuss. I'm quite uninjured."

The duke ignored her as the butler left. He moved to a sideboard where he poured out a glass of brandy for himself. "I'm glad you aren't any worse for wear."

"As am I." In fact, she did feel like a heroine in need of rescue, which is exactly what the duke had done. Another tiny piece of her heart went unexpectedly into his keeping.

In short order, the housekeeper brought in a tea service on a silver tray that she laid next to the first one on the table. "Oh, dearie, you had a narrow escape."

"She did indeed," Barr murmured. He brought over a whisky bottle then added a small measure into her teacup once the housekeeper poured out a serving. "No protests. It will calm your nerves."

"That it will, Your Grace." Mrs. Braxton pressed a cool cloth to Cate's forehead. "You are a bit flushed, so what you've been through must have been quite exciting."

Did she refer to the mirror crashing or the wild coupling

she'd shared with the duke not an hour past? Regardless, she refused to look at him for fear they would give themselves away. Instead, she peered up into the housekeeper's face. "I appreciate your tending to me." In fact, the coolness from the wet cloth felt heavenly on her skin. "But I'm fine. Truly." When she took a sip from her tea, she coughed from the addition of the whiskey. "God, that's horrible."

Both the duke and Mrs. Braxton chuckled.

Barr flashed a grin. "You learn to develop a taste for it." He winked. "I'll call for my carriage. Perhaps it's best to take up the task of translation tomorrow. Today has been far too exciting, I think."

That was an understatement.

CHAPTER TEN

December 21, 1816

"OUT WITH IT, Travers. I know you're fairly bursting to say something." Barr wasn't in any sort of mood that morning, for it was once again raining and due to Cate's schedule at the lending library, he wouldn't see her until teatime.

His valet remained partially hidden in the wardrobe, apparently trying to select a waistcoat. "Why do you suppose that?"

Barr snorted. "Because you have been the one to harangue me about putting myself back out into society. From his perch on a chair in his dressing room, he tugged on first one boot and then the other.

"Well, there is that." Travers came away from the wardrobe with a silver satin waistcoat in hand, embroidered with black swirls. Yet a grin flirted about his mouth as held approached with the garment. "However, that doesn't matter just now."

"Oh?" He shoved himself to his feet then held out his arms for Travers to slip the waistcoat onto his frame. "Why?"

"Because there has been a shift in you."

"Gammon."

"There has been, and I can't believe you haven't seen it in yourself, or at the very least felt it." One of Travers' blond eyebrows rose in challenge before he went behind Barr's back to tighten the laces. "And after we all took tea together yesterday while decorating the drawing room, one of the maids said you went into the library alone with Miss Pickwick. With the door closed."

Well, damn.

Heat crept up the back of his neck. "That is true. I wanted to show her the rare first editions my father and I managed to collect. I closed the door to shield where I put them from prying eyes."

"While I believe that, I also believe you and she shared something... else while in that room." He brought out a jacket of sapphire superfine. "We have been friends for a long time, Your Grace. Tell me the truth. Have you finally bedded Miss Pickwick?"

If he didn't answer the question, Travers would continue to harp on it until he finally broke. With a sigh, Barr nodded. "I did, though there wasn't a bed involved in the true sense of the word." As he spoke, he couldn't help but offer a little grin. "What began as a bit of teasing on the library ladder soon became so much more." Now that he'd started confessing, he couldn't stop. "First on the sofa then against one of the bookshelves."

The payoff was more than he could have hoped for as Travers gawked at him, the jacket dangling from his fingers. "I see."

"It's not often I'm able to render you speechless." Feeling far too cheeky, Barr took the jacket from his valet and then shoved his arms into the sleeves. "Don't you have a comment or advice?"

Travers cleared his throat. "I'm stunned you have advanced the relationship in that way."

"Ah, because you didn't think I had the courage?"

"That's not it, but after what you'd shared with her before yesterday, I assumed that was all there would happen between you." A slow grin spread across his face. "Did you, uh, enjoy yourself? You weren't ridden with guilt?"

Another flood of heat went up his neck as he manipulated the buttons on his jacket. "I did enjoy myself, and no, guilt didn't figure into any of it."

"I'm impressed." He held out a hand, and when Barr clasped

it, they shook. "Do you think you might develop feelings for her eventually?"

"Over and above desire and lust?" He shrugged. "I don't know." Then another thought occurred to him, and a gasp escaped him. "Do you mean for marriage purposes?" After what they'd done together, should he at least consider it? Was she even now pregnant? And if she was, did that necessitate marriage?

Of course he knew the answer, and he wasn't the sort of man to leave her in scandal and shame. If she fell pregnant, he would find some way to convince the willful woman that they should wed, and that the child would be far better off with them both around than not.

Travers shrugged. "I wouldn't know, but *do* you have any softer feelings for her?"

"Uh…" Though he admired how self-assured Cate was, how forthright, how her mind worked, how compassionate she was when caring for her father, did any of that mean he was in love with her? No, it did not, but he trusted and respected her, and the heated connection between them was far too difficult to ignore. He didn't know all that much about her. However, he desperately wanted to. "She certainly makes my life more interesting."

"An understatement." But Travers frowned. "And you look forward to seeing her each day? I mean, this morning, you're fairly vibrating in your own skin with anticipation."

Barr ignored his friend's question in order to wander to a mirror mounted on the wall, in the same as the one that nearly fell on her in the library. He adjusted the knot of his cravat and the folds of the fabric. "As you've said before, I need to spend time with others. Her translation of the Egyptian book is coming along. I don't wish to interrupt that work, but I also don't want to miss out on each new passage she uncovers."

"I'll wager that's not all you wish to uncover of her," the valet said with a cheeky wink.

"Do shut up, Travers." Yet he couldn't summon annoyance, for what he'd said was true. "You're not wrong. I've yet to see her completely nude." God, was he a cad for speaking that aloud?

The valet shared a knowing glance with him. "More's the pity, hmm?" When Barr didn't answer, Travers continued. "That must mean something."

"Not necessarily."

"Don't speak gammon, Your Grace. It's perfectly acceptable if you wish to pursue other things with the woman beyond the translation."

"Oh, I know that. It just feels... different than my last relationship." In fact, since her schedule wouldn't align with his until the evening, the feeling of missing her persisted.

"Of course it will. She isn't the same as Her Grace was, and there is nothing wrong with that." Travers brushed away some lint from one of Barr's sleeves. "Miss Pickwick was impressed when I showed her some of the renovations you've done. I don't think she could believe you did them yourself without help."

"No doubt you told her I was stubborn."

"I'm sure she has already discerned that, You Grace."

Barr pulled a face. "Regardless, I'm glad I made an impression."

"In more than a few ways, eh?"

God, was everything an innuendo with him? He shook his head and fought off the heat moving up his neck. "That's enough, Travers. Have some respect." Of course, if he'd followed his own advice, he wouldn't have bedded her or trifled with her in any way. "Regardless, I'm not sure how to go forward with her in *any* capacity, let alone continue with what we already have."

Did he want more? There was no way to untangle his thoughts just now.

Travers shrugged. "Perhaps you should share your hopes for the future with her."

"I have, to a certain extent." Except when they'd spoken yesterday of that very thing, most of the answers and talking had hinged on her answers... He frowned as he peered at his friend. "*Do* I have dreams or goals for the future, though? I merely wish to live out the rest of my days in contentment; to do all the things I didn't have time to do when rearing children and having all my focus on the title."

"Everyone has dreams, Your Grace. Even you." Travers laid a comforting hand on Barr's shoulder. "Consider that the difficult portion of your life is over. Now you're coming into the time that you can court fun and excitement. After all, you're not dead yet."

"You keep telling me that."

"It's no less true."

Slowly, Barr nodded. "Since the advent of Miss Pickwick, I've felt more alive than ever before." The admission didn't surprise him, for it had pressed upon his consciousness over the past couple of days.

"Then why shouldn't you make your interest known? If she feels the same, even better."

Shock went through his chest. "You are suggesting that I officially court her?"

"Or..." The valet shrugged. "You could straight out marry her."

"I don't know." The thought of marrying again, of taking on that sort of responsibility when life was so fragile sent icy shivers down his spine. He shook his head. "It's... complicated. Miss Pickwick is not of the *beau monde* or even the *ton*."

"What difference does that make? You were married before. You have your heir, and soon your son will have children. The line is secure. Why not marry for pleasure this time, for joy, for the adventure of it?"

For long moments, Barr thought over those words. They danced in his mind, shimmering and glittering with tempting promise. The idea held a certain merit... or perhaps he was merely depraved after all. "Does that discount what I had with my wife, though?"

"Of course not, but *that* union was based in duty and responsibility even if you loved her." Travers' expression showed nothing but earnestness. "Now you can be free and enjoy your life without the stress of what you had with Her Grace."

"I've never looked at it that way before." It was a bit… freeing. "However, I don't know if Miss Pickwick wishes to marry. She's made it known she will only do so for love, yet the idea of only having her as a mistress doesn't sit well with me." He frowned as his thoughts continued to swirl. "Having a mistress isn't as enticing as men make it seem, for Miss Pickwick could marry someone else despite what she and I get up to…"

"And you'll lose her."

"Indeed, before I can make up *my* mind." The longer he stared at his valet, the more he couldn't manage to tamp that thought down. It was frightening in that he was rather more attached to Cate than he probably should be. And the thought of having her in his life in some capacity after the translation was completed appealed to him. But he couldn't dawdle. "Travers, I've decided I'm going out this afternoon."

"Oh? Where?" Then a sly expression came over his face. "To the lending library?"

"Perhaps." Heat rose up the back of his neck once again. "Or perhaps to the shops. I have gifts to procure, in any event, for Christmas, so I won't know where I'm going until I arrive."

But *something* needed to be done.

AFTER POPPING INTO more than a few shops despite the rain and then realizing he'd chosen gifts for nearly everyone on his staff, his children, his mother, as well as something for Cate—would she even like a fan with Mother-of-Pearl spine and a pair of embroidered white silk stockings?—he finally alighted from his carriage in front of the lending library off Fleet Street.

To his driver, he said, "If you'll wait, I shouldn't be more than an hour, if that." He didn't know if Cate would have time to talk with him. Not to mention this might be a stupid idea and make him look like a nodcock, but he couldn't leave things up to chance.

Could he?

"Very well, Your Grace. I'll just go to the nearest mews. The rain makes for a horrid afternoon. I'll come back 'round in an hour."

Barr nodded. "I agree. Stay as dry as you can." Then he went up the pavement a few feet before going inside the circulating library.

It was quite a busy day with patrons everywhere. No doubt everyone was driven nearly mad from the rain and were desperate for new reading material, but he easily located Cate. For a bit, he contented himself with watching her as he pretended to peruse the shelves.

Was she always that lovely and composed? Her brown hair caught in a low bun only served to call attention to her slender neck. As she spoke quietly with a female patron, her eyes shone with the clear love she had for books, and her hands were animated as she drew the lady toward a shelf that no doubt held her recommendations. Barr moved along the shelf so he could keep Cate in his sight. Again today, she wore a simple dress in a navy hue. How much better would she appear in bright colors and expensive fabrics? He could almost imagine jewels winking at her throat and wrists. Could he be the man that might provide all of that for her?

Would he? Was it something she would even entertain from him?

Not knowing, he crept away into the lounge, for it appeared she would be with the patron for some moments more. Might as well order tea and wait for a better time when she might be free. But before he could ask for a table, a footman, clearly in a hurry and carrying a loaded silver tray with the detritus of someone else's repast, barreled around a corner and ran straight into him.

"Well, damn," he said, for there was no time to say more or dodge out of the way.

Dishes crashed to the floor in a cacophony of sound. Leftover tea splashed from an overturned pot to splatter all over the front of him. Small bowls of jam and clotted cream upended onto his greatcoat and left sticky, wet streaks behind. A piece of sponge cake stuck to his lapel while lumps of sugar fell upon his boots like icy snow.

"I am so sorry," the footman said with eyes wide with fear as he reached for the cake and quickly whisked it onto the tray he remarkably still held onto.

"Don't worry about it. Accidents happened." But that was his favorite greatcoat, and now there was jam staining a portion of his superfine jacket beneath. Hot anger simmered just beneath the surface of his skin. Truly, the footman should have been paying more attention.

"Good heavens!" A woman from one of the back rooms of the lounge, presumably the kitchen, and she rushed over to him with a rag in hand. "Let me help, Your Grace."

At least *someone* recognized him.

As the woman tried to dab at the mess decorating the front of him, he waved her away while the footman kneeled to put the scattered and broken pieces of crockery and china onto his tray. "Leave me be. I shall take care of it." As he spoke, he scrubbed the worst of the mess with his handkerchief.

Then none of it mattered, for Cate came into the room. She gazed at him with rounded eyes and amusement in her expression.

"My goodness, what a picture you make, Scarborough."

"I imagine I do." He offered her what felt like a goofy grin. "I'd hoped to take tea and perhaps ask you to join me, but I caused a scene instead."

"It was clearly my fault," the footman said as he rose to his feet, clutching the tray with shaking hands. "I will pay for a new coat if you wish it, Your Grace."

That was almost laughable, for no doubt the greatcoat cost as much as what the poor fellow made in an annual salary, but he took pity on the young man. "There is no need for that. My housekeeper and laundress can perform miracles upon occasion. I'm certain it will be as right as rain before long."

He hoped. In the grand scheme of things, it was only an outer garment. There were far more important subjects to worry over.

Cate laid a hand briefly on his sleeve, and his attention was completely distracted by her presence. "You poor thing," she said beneath her breath. "Come with me." To the woman standing ineffectually with the stained rag in her hand, she asked, "Could you see that His Grace is given a tea tray? I'm sure it will set his mind at ease to have a cuppa."

"Of course, Miss Pickwick."

As the woman quickly walked back to the kitchen, Cate led him to a table near a window. She ushered him into a chair so that his back faced the bulk of the room, perhaps to shield him from curious eyes and whispers behind hands.

"You have quite the knack for making an entrance." Once she drew a lace-edged handkerchief from her reticule, she helped him clean his coat as best she could. Then she slipped into the chair across the small table from him. "I have but a half hour for a break, but I'll happily join you and keep you company while you take tea."

"I would appreciate that." Just being in her presence and having the faint floral scent of her teased his nose made him feel more relaxed than he had in a long while. Of course, because she was so close, and her touch as she scrubbed at his clothing sent interest shivering into his shaft. It was pure insanity how much— and how often—he wanted her, but there was nothing for it. "At this point, I'll take whatever time you'll give me, however you'll concede it."

She sat back with her gaze resting on his face as she folded her handkerchief. "If you are hoping to use flattery on me, it won't work."

"Oh." He couldn't help but frown. "Why not?" Truly, the world of trying to woo a woman was damned confusing at times.

"Because I already look forward to seeing you."

When she smiled, his world tilted, and he forgot all about the sticky patch on one cuff of his coat and how his jacket smelled like raspberry. Did that mean he well on his way to being tip over tail for her? That remained to be seen, but life was certainly better when she was there.

"Ah, that is lovely to hear."

Cate nodded. "Also, I'm anxious to return to my translation work, so if you could stretch out your tea for a bit and then perhaps browse about for another hour, you could escort me back to your townhouse. Unless, of course, you'd rather put off the work until tomorrow?"

"Since I'm anxious to know how the book ends, I shall do whatever it takes to wait for you." Both to finish her shift at the lending library and for whatever else she needed.

God, what a nodcock I'm turning into.

"Excellent." She patted his hand and then tucked her handkerchief into her reticule as a different footman from before brought out tea on a tray. "If all goes well, I might have the translation finished by Christmas."

And then what? Would their association come to an end? The lovely peace he'd found from sitting down with her fled in the face of panic and cold worry.

What the devil am I going to do?

CHAPTER ELEVEN

December 22, 1816
No 12 Hanover Square
Mayfair, London

B Y THE TIME Cate was on her second cup of tea, her father made an appearance in the morning room.

"Good morning, Papa. Did you have a late night?" As she asked the question, the longcase clock at the other end of the corridor chimed the eleventh hour of the morning.

"I did. I'm afraid I was lost on a tangent of research." When he joined her at the table, a footman rushed over with a pot of coffee, a cup, and a plate full of her father's favorite breakfast foods. "Time well spent, though."

"How is your paper coming along?"

"Quite well. My notes are scattered, of course, but I'm satisfied with the project." He slid her a glance. "It would go faster if you were helping me with organization, but I understand you're busy with your own endeavors."

She nodded and told herself she wouldn't be pulled in by guilt. "My work at the lending library as well as the translation is occupying all my time just now, but you are fully capable of writing your paper without my help."

"I think you mother and I raised you to be slightly too independent," he said with the hint of a grin as he poured out a cup of coffee. "That is both a good and a bad thing."

"You are once more thinking of my future." It wasn't a question, for she knew it weighed heavily on his shoulders.

"How can I not?" With the wave of a hand, her father dismissed the footman who hovered near the sideboard. Then he settled his gaze squarely on her. "There is something different about you these days, my girl."

"Nonsense." Cate shook her head though her cheeks heated. Would he notice the blush? "I'm the same as I have ever been, just being pulled in different directions. Which reminds me, I should probably go by the shops soon for Christmas presents."

"Don't try to distract me, pet. I'm telling you. There is a different air about you these days." One of his graying eyebrows rose in challenge. "Why is that, I wonder, and why is it that this change has happened shortly after you met the Duke of Scarborough?"

Oh, dear.

"I'll admit, he is as interesting as the translation work I'm doing for him." In fact, she'd dreamed about both last night, especially after how endearing he'd been yesterday in the library lounge after the poor luck with the tea tray. Was that a product of the alleged curse from the Egyptian book?

"Hmm." For the next several moments, her father ate in silence while Cate finished her cup of tea. Then, as he dabbed at the corners of his mouth with his linen napkin, he spoke again. "I have known you all your life, poppet, and I also know your penchant of chasing the wrong men for the wrong reasons."

"Oh, Papa, please don't—"

"I must." He laid his napkin upon his lap. "After your last position as a governess, you were let go after having an amorous relationship with your employer. Are you going down the same path with the duke? Will you have your heart broken again?" When she remained quiet, he sighed. "Are you more than a mere translator for Scarborough? Is that why you have been so happy as of late?"

Well, how could she deny it? Her father may be many things,

but he was a keen observer when he wanted to be. "Oh, Papa, it's… confusing at best."

"Only the best stories are, pet. Now, why don't you tell me what is happening."

She heaved out a sigh. "From the first, there has been some sort of aggressive and quite breathtaking connection between us."

"And you acted upon that connection?" There was no judgment in his tones, merely curiosity.

"I'm afraid he acted upon it first, and then I returned the favor, until…"

Her father held up a hand. "I don't need to know."

"Ah, good." How much should she tell her father? Perhaps he could provide insight. "All of that to say I am currently at sixes and sevens because of him."

"How so?"

"Well, I…" She briefly held her bottom lip between her teeth. "I'm not sure but I am starting to develop softer feelings for him over and above desire and attraction. And, I'm not quite certain what I should do about it."

"Do you believe the duke feels the same?"

"I wouldn't know. He doesn't discuss such things with me, and I only see him a few hours a day while working on the translation."

"Mmm." Her father refreshed his coffee cup. "So after you finish the translation, you feel that the two of you will go your separate ways?"

"I expect so." Cate shrugged. "There is nothing else there, don't you think? Over and above what we've shared, there is no future. He is a duke; I am the daughter of a university professor, not even a member of the *ton*."

Never had she given much stock in social status before, but knowing there was a vast world of difference between her and the duke? It was almost as heartbreaking as knowing she would soon pass out of his life. An ache set up around her heart. How uttering depressing that was.

"I'm of the opinion that none of it matters. People are people. It is the world, society, that puts weigh on position and titles or the lack thereof." He took a few sips of coffee before speaking again. "I also think you have already answered your own question."

She frowned. "How so?" With an effort, she forced her concentration back on him.

"If you are nearly gutted that you'll not see him again after your paid position finishes, then I think you know that there are definitely feelings there."

"And if there are? What good will they do? He has his life, and I have mine." She shrugged, tried to pretend she didn't care. "Once this horrible weather pattern changes and life can go back to a somewhat methodical rhythm, he will take up the reins of his life as a duke, and perhaps that is as it should be."

Catherine, you are such a liar!

"Hmm, I rather think you're hiding, but it's early days yet. Let us see how things develop over the Christmastide season, then we'll talk again."

"I don't know what good that will have. Nothing will change." Another sigh escaped her. "I need to dress for the day. The duke is expecting me around one o'clock, and since I made a bit of headway on the translation yesterday afternoon, I'm hoping to keep that momentum."

Seeing Barr and interacting with him was an added boon.

Combes House
Grosvenor Square, Mayfair
London

CATE HAD BEEN working on the translation in the duke's study for a couple of hours. When she took a short break to rest her eyes and to stretch her cramped limbs, it was then that a loud thudding sound reached her ears followed by a masculine groan.

"What in the world?" After springing up from the chair behind the desk, she dashed out of the room. "Barr?"

"I'm here… more or less," came his slightly muffled answer.

She frowned as she sought him out, and when she discovered him sprawled on the second-floor landing, a gasp left her throat. Quickly making her way to him, she kneeled by his side. "Are you hurt? Is there anything broken?"

"You mean over and above my pride?" He maneuvered into a sitting position with another groan. "I don't think so. Just fell down the damned stairs."

"Did you trip?" She glanced up the staircase, but didn't see anything amiss.

"I don't know. I don't believe there was anything on the treads. It must have been the curse."

"What?" That took her by surprise. "Curse?" Then she snorted. "Have you been talking to Travers?"

"Yes." A chuckle mixed with a groan followed as he struggled to his feet with her assistance. "Did he also warn you about a curse tied to that book?"

"He did." Her frown deepened. "Do you think it's true?"

"It's difficult to say." With a hand to his hip, he walked slowly and stiffly toward the drawing room. "There was the mirror and the tea tray fiasco from yesterday…"

"Now this," she added in a soft voice.

"Yes, but I'm none of the worse for wear. There will be bruises on the morrow, I'm afraid."

"That can't be helped, I suppose." With a sense of whimsy, she put an arm about his waist and helped him into the drawing room. "I hope your ancient body will heal in a timely manner."

"I'm cut to the quick, Miss Pickwick," he said with mock horror in his voice.

How could she not grin? "Come on." After seeing him settled on a low sofa, she peered down at him. "Should I fetch a compress or salve or willowbark tea?"

"No." He caught her hand and tugged her down with him. "Stay with me." Then he situated her onto the sofa with his legs framing her body and her back against his chest.

Surprise twisted with excitement down her spine. "You're flirting with scandal since the door is open."

"I doubt that. It's Sunday. The servants have the day off." The rumble of his laughter sent an avalanche of tingles through her chest. "It's only you and I here until dawn. Dinner is cold cuts, cheese, and bread left in the kitchen, and soup should I care to warm it on the stove." The warmth of his breath skated over her cheek. "One of my favorite things each week."

"Ah." As the steady rain beat against the windows and the candles flickered in their silver holders around the room, coupled with the fire snapping behind the ornamental screen in the hearth, it was far too cozy. Suddenly, she didn't have the strength to protest or even leave the secure circle of his arms. "Very well."

"Good." He brushed his lips over her nape, chuckling when she shivered. "How is the translation coming?"

"Slowly. Once I have another few pages finished, I'll tell you another chunk of the tale."

"I can hardly wait." As he spoke, the duke caressed her arms, her neck, her shoulders, her nape. "It's strange, but I'm quite invested in a couple's romance who lived thousands of years before we are now."

"I know what you mean." With a frown, Cate glanced at him over her shoulder for his hands were roaming over various other portions of her body to leave trails of heat behind. "What are you about, Scarborough?"

His eyes darkened to deep sapphire. "Seeking to soothe my aches by sending you through your paces." As he spoke, he yanked down the bodice of her dress. Seconds later, the under-clothes were manipulated enough that he easily freed her breasts. "Unless you are not of the same mind?"

Dear God, how could she not be, when half her thoughts revolved around having his hands on her person and his body heaving against hers? "I would enjoy that very much, actually."

"Excellent, for every time you speak of that damned book, I find myself wanting you even more than usual."

"Oh!" Tingles shot through her core. He was quite potent even after a tumble down a portion of the stairs. "If you think you can manage pleasuring a woman after your fall, then I look forward to it." She again glanced at him. "When will you begin your seduction?"

"Immediately, of course, or could you not already guess that?" Barr nuzzled the crook of her shoulder and at the same time, he lightly danced his fingers over her breasts, slowly, oh so slowly, bringing her nipples into tight buds.

"Don't be an arse, Your Grace." The words sneaked out upon the wings of a moan. Her back arched of its own accord, which put her bosom more firmly into his hands.

He chuckled. Using his palms, he caressed those sensitive buds, brought them into a frenzy that had pleasure zipping between them and her core. Need pulsed at the apex of her thighs, and no matter how much she wanted him to take her in a firmer grip, he never did. Merely continued to tease with the lightest of touches. As he worked, he hummed a series of notes from a popular waltz, and he continued to concentrate on bringing her to the brink of pleasure through her breasts alone.

"You are going to toss me over just like this, aren't you?"

"If I can manage it." His low-pitched laughter sent gooseflesh rippling over her skin. With his lips at her nape, Barr teased her breasts, her nipples all over again, and this time, the friction and roughness from the callouses on his fingers added another layer of bliss to the play.

"Oh, oh!" Cate let her eyes shutter closed, and once more her back arched. Need throbbed through her body while her breath came in shallow pants. Blissful sensations darted over her skin. Fires lit in her blood. Remarkably, she was nearly at that edge, hovering, waiting, seconds away from flying; it was as if his hands were magic. "More," she gasped out and lifted a hand to wrap around his nape, encourage his head closer to hers. "Give me more."

"Like that, do you?"

Before she could comment on the tinge of arrogance in his voice, he drew up her skirts and then his hand was between her thighs, his fingers burrowing through her curls. Always skilled, he strummed those talented digits along her flesh, back and forth, and when she whimpered, put a hand over his to guide him to where she needed him to be most, he found her swollen button, encouraged it out of hiding, and then applied friction to that nubbin as if that was his only purpose in life.

Perhaps it was in this moment.

Shivery sensations raced along her spine, pushed into every nerve ending. She held his hand tight to her pearl, clutched his nape with her other hand. He kissed her neck but didn't leave off with his frenzied friction, glided his lips over her cheek, and when he bit her earlobe, streaks of need slammed through her core to heighten the feelings already crashing through her body.

This was a more intense version of the duke, and she rather enjoyed it. So much so that she squirmed in her position between his splayed legs. The hard ridge of his arousal pressed against her bottom. "I'm nearly there..." Oh, she couldn't concentrate on words, and if he didn't finish her, she'd melt into a puddle.

"Then let me help you over." The dratted man pinched her nipple, rolled that hardened tip. The pleasure-pain sent her hurtling toward that glimmering edge. His chuckle was all too satisfied as he increased the pressure. "Don't fight it, Catherine. Let me see you come undone, watch your face as you find pleasure."

Those words made her shatter, and the more she relaxed into his care, the greater the wave of bliss smacked into her, picked her up, and then carried her into that void where sound and light didn't exist. Cate cried out her bliss since they were alone. She writhed against him, held his hand tighter to her button while familiar contractions pulsed through her core.

Eventually, she came back to herself with only enough strength to slump against him. "Your potency from two days ago wasn't a fluke."

"That is good to know." He nuzzled the crook of her shoulder again before he eased her off his lap. "But I'm not nearly done with you."

"What does that mean?" As much as she wanted to give into the lethargy setting into her limbs, she wanted him to finish her by coupling. "I'd hoped you would continue."

"Oh, I will. Don't worry there." He gained his feet while manipulating the buttons of his front falls. "I want to try one of the positions from the book."

"What?" Anticipation spiraled through her belly to mix with the desire and hungry longing he'd already awoken. "Which one?"

"Nothing too insane or dangerous." When his engorged length tumbled out of his breeches, she couldn't help but stare and moisten her lips. What was it about his man that made her throw caution to the wind and abandon all common sense?

"How about I just tease you with my mouth?"

"Not right now." Batting away her hands, the duke encouraged her onto her hands and knees facing the back of the sofa. "Put your hands on the frame. Pretend it's a bamboo screen and that we are in the heart of Egypt inside a pharaoh's palace and that we can be discovered at any moment." His hands were everywhere. "Spread your legs and stick your arse out." Then he assisted her into the position and shoved her skirts up to her waist. "You've tempted me beyond reason." The command in his graveled voice sent shivers down her spine.

"But I haven't done anything."

"You have done much, merely by being you, and that makes this all the more confusing and arousing."

"Oh!" Cate did as requested, but she glanced over her shoulder at him. "I rather like this forceful side of you." It sent tingles between her thighs, brought her to the edge of bliss before he'd even manipulated any of her sensitive bits.

"You bring it out in me," he all but growled. "Catch me against the edge until I have no choice but to act. In your company, I am no longer the man I was before, and as you drag me from every bit of security I've known, I'm not sure who I'll ultimately grow into."

"Is that a bad thing?" It felt all too lovely to know she'd been a catalyst into helping him change, even if he'd not wanted to.

"God, no. I should act the gentleman, but I find it's impossible where you're concerned." He gripped her hips while she splayed her legs, and he fit his wide tip to her opening.

"Perhaps this is the man you should have been all along. Besides, I never said with conviction that I wanted a decent—Ah!"

He thrust into her passage with such authority and went so deeply they both groaned with appreciation. Her eyes crossed as intense pleasure danced through her body. "Oh, goodness," she managed to gasp while shifting her stance into something more comfortable. "What else have you got, Scarborough? Enough to challenge the young man in the Egyptian book?"

"Let's see." Every time he penetrated her channel, he went deep, oh so deep. His shaft rubbed against the swollen nubbin at her center, enhancing the need he'd already invoked. His hold on her hips was hard enough that he'd probably leave marks on her skin. Oddly enough, she craved that souvenir. "This will go fast. I can't sustain momentum."

She was lost to the madness he created. "Then make it unforgettable." Her knuckles were white as she gripped the high-backed wooden frame of the sofa. A low moan released from her when he slammed into her. "This is… this is… Oh please, don't be gentle. I don't want that from you right now." At least then her thoughts surrounding him might solidify.

"But a gentleman should never—"

As if this was the stance of a gentleman! "For the love of everything holy, Barrington, claim me as if we've run out of time." Then she went silent, biting her bottom lip, for his next push nearly hurtled her over the edge toward bliss.

"Fuck, there's a part of me that *really* wants to make you beg."

A new round of heat went through her for a far different reason. "Perhaps another time." Would he not get on with it?

"A promise for certain." But he soon found a rhythm, dug his fingers into her hips for greater purchase, and apparently set out to send her to the heights of pleasure with alacrity and conviction.

Over and over, he slammed into her, giving her exactly what she'd asked him for. It was heady stuff, addicting as researching ancient worlds, perhaps even better, and she couldn't have enough. "I need more," she gasped, lifting her head, and looking at him from over her shoulder. Pure pleasure lined his face, and he was the most handsome man she'd ever seen. "I want to feel all of you, unabandoned and without restraint."

He renewed his grip on her hips, yanking her toward him, and she pushed back to feel the full effect of him inside her.

"Yes, Barr, yes!"

Deeper he stroked. Faster he moved while the thunder growled. This coupling had nothing to do with emotions or thoughts of the future. It was raw, real, and based only in mutual need and primal passion. The sound of flesh hitting flesh echoed in her ears blending with the sound of the rain against the windows. Her breasts bounced from the exercise. Heat engulfed her and still he thrust while she bucked her hips against him, meeting each one with her own power, which sent him ever deeper.

When he snaked his free hand around her hips to rub his fingers over her button, her control shattered. "Yes, hurry!"

"What the devil do you think I'm doing?" He followed the question by a series of deep, oh so impossibly deep and hard, teeth-shatteringly hard thrusts that sought to separate her soul from her body. "Cate, please…"

"I'm there." White light moved up to meet her as she fell over the edge and tumbled, hurtled really, into an intense release.

A keening cry pulled from her throat, and she was so glad the servants weren't in residence. It was all she could do to hold onto the back of the sofa as he continued to spear into her. Her core convulsed frantically around his member. Seconds later, Barr hit release in spectacular fashion, for he shouted out her name, buried himself in her passage while tugging her tight to his body. His shaft jerked and pulsed, and her body milked him dry.

Dear God, they couldn't keep doing this, for there was most certainly a risk to her especially if they never took precautions, but oh, despite the worry she wouldn't trade these moments for any sort of security.

"Bloody hell that was powerful, almost bordered on madness," he whispered and wrapped his arms around her. His breathing was as ragged as hers. "I had no idea I could come that splendidly."

Oh, he was adorable. So easily she could—*Don't even think it, Cate!* "Agreed. You nearly killed me." She laughed, but it was a shaky affair. Exhaustion clung to the sound. "It was quite wonderful, and I rather think you've spoiled me for anyone else." It was as close as she could go to admitting to feelings she couldn't begin to puzzle out at the moment.

A soft growl issued from him. "Good, because I don't believe I could share." The duke pulled away, severing their intimate connection. Immediately, she missed his warmth, his solid form against hers. Then he collapsed onto the sofa with her, arranging their bodies so that they laid next to each other.

Cate drooped beside him, curled into his body as residual tremors still flitted through her form. "Thank goodness it's a Sunday." As much as she enjoyed that coupling, there had to be more to her existence than sex and slaking carnal need with this man.

No matter how satisfying.

For both of them.

CHAPTER TWELVE

*D*EAR GOD.

That coupling had taken much from him, and it had also surprised the hell out of him. Barr didn't care, for not only was he perfectly content to lie with her on the sofa, but he also wondered what was wrong with him that he apparently couldn't keep his hands off this woman.

The scent of her perfume haunted his mind with the hints of vanilla and floral. They would forever remind him of her if she should ever move out of his life. Beyond that, the softness of her skin, the sounds of her breathing, the flutter of her pulse beneath her skin, the way the brown arc of her lashes against her cheeks all worked toward fascination that bordered on obsession. Damn, but when was the last time that happened to him?

Perhaps he was touched in the head or half to being senile. Perhaps something wasn't quite right with his brain; he couldn't remember a time when he'd been this compelled to join physically with a woman, and one he'd only just met a handful of days ago.

Was this what happened when a man grew older? Did it mean the end was near?

Then all those thoughts cleared. More likely, he feared he might like her more than he should, but surely it was merely due to all the physical pleasures they'd been sharing. Love didn't happen that quickly.

Did it?

Of course not. *Don't be an arse, Scarborough.* He tightened his arm about Cate's hip as she lightly dozed. What he felt for her wasn't love.

Was it? Could he envision his future with her in it in some capacity? That required more thought than he had energy for, so he contented himself with holding her and enjoying the moment.

But damn, this was certainly the height of scandal, and it couldn't last. That was the reality of things.

"I can almost hear you thinking, Scarborough." Cate's statement was a bit muffled, for her head rested on his upper chest near the folds of his cravat. "Please don't ruin this moment with worry. What's done is done, and that's the end."

He frowned. "Does that mean you aren't enjoying what we've shared thus far?"

"Absolutely not. Though I am still annoyed that I haven't seen you fully nude." She rose up on an elbow to better meet his gaze, and the cheeky grin she gave him had the power to turn his world upside down.

"There is that, but I could say the same of you." Now that the idea of seeing her *sans* clothing was in his mind, he couldn't evict it. Renewed interest shivered through his shaft. Lifting a hand, he let his fingertips drift over her cheek, and the warmth of her nearly had him shivering with need.

Her eyes darkened from his touch. "Do stop looking at me like that, for you will surely kill me with all this exercise. Not that I mind, for I have never had a lover of your particular appetite." She briefly pressed her lips to his in a kiss he could easily get lost in. When she pulled back, a pretty blush stained her cheeks. "Beyond that, you have managed to surprise me at every turn, not merely with your carnal prowess." There was nothing but honesty in her eyes, and there was a moment when he felt he would drown in those rich brown depths. "I am discovering that you are interesting in your own right."

"Well, that is good to know."

"Why you try to hide that, I have no idea. It is perfectly acceptable for a duke to have other interests beyond his title and duties to parliament." She dropped her hand to his chest, and the muscles in his abdomen clenched with anticipation.

"Ah, well, perhaps I am a slow learner." Yet what did he truly know about *her*? Perhaps it was time to have a personal talk that had nothing to do with tumbling into bed. Or rather onto whatever piece of furniture was nearby and available since they'd not yet managed to seek out a bed. God, what would she look like draped over his desk in this study?

What the hell is wrong with me?

Perhaps nothing. Was this his natural personality coming out, thanks to her encouragement? It was too early in the conversation to say for a fact.

Never had he been like that when married to his wife. He'd conducted himself like a proper gentleman, bedded his wife behind closed doors in the suite they'd shared, had intercourse once a week depending on their combined schedules, and generally presented themselves as a proper couple of the *beau monde*. For the whole course of his marriage, they'd been staid and consistent in every aspect. They had been the typical societal couple and had done what had been expected of them.

Yet with Cate, there was none of that. Being with her was frantic, electric, explosive. There was nothing staid or scheduled about her or them together. With her, he felt as if he were continuously falling down the stairs or being thrown off a cliff, barely able to catch his breath, and he couldn't wait to have his hands on her body, couple with her as if he was naught but an animal.

It didn't mean one or the other of the relationships were wrong, it just meant they were different and allowed him to explore different sides of himself.

Outside that, he admired how Cate's mind worked, how she was able to puzzle through the symbols and drawings and other text of that Ancient Egyptian book.

What else was she about? There was a craving deep inside him to learn everything about her so that his brain might catch up with his body in being lost.

She watched him with a sleepy, sated expression, and all he wanted to do with kiss her. "You are once more lost in thought, aren't you?"

"A bit, yes." He gave her what he hoped was a wry grin. "I have been since we met, I think."

"Such gammon. There is nothing special about me to warrant that." But her smile and the way her eyes lit said otherwise.

"I think you have no idea." Then it was his turn to gently press his lips to hers.

The longer he laid on that sofa with her, the more he feared they would linger in the library for purposes that had nothing to do with a translation. While he wanted nothing more than to use himself up in the pursuit of pleasure with her, there needed to be something else between them, else that passion would burn out and they would be left with nothing.

And that was something he couldn't contemplate.

Moving off the sofa, he quickly stuffed his flagging length into his breeches and then did up the buttons of his front falls. "Come walk with me."

She frowned as she sat up then fussed with putting her clothing to rights and tucking her charms away. "Where? It's raining."

"In the garden for a bit. Perhaps around the square." He shrugged. "Does it matter? I'm bored of being stuck in the house all the time. I need a different perspective." Perhaps it would help to clear his head so he could make sense of what was happening between him and Cate.

"Um… I suppose that would be all right, as long as we bring umbrellas. If my clothing is too wet, I'll need to go home early before I can finish today's pages."

"Fair enough." He nodded. Above everything, he didn't wish to forfeit this fleeting time with her from today. "I promise you won't become too wet." Unless he took an unplanned foray between her thighs. Then he could easily find out just how wet she could be…

Good God, Scarborough. You are headed to Bedlam for certain.

Ten minutes later saw them in the back garden, and with him in his top hat and greatcoat and Cate wearing her pelisse and bonnet, both carrying umbrellas, he led her into the square beyond the garden.

As the drum of the rain on the umbrella's surface muffled the rest of the world, he strolled at her side while avoiding puddles or dodgy-looking muddy areas.

"Regarding what you and I just got up to…"

"Do stop, Barr. I don't want to hear your speech full of obligation or rambling gratitude. We came together. We gave into passion. There is nothing more to tell." She shook her head as they walked side by side. "I allow you to have access to my body because I enjoy carnal endeavors and couplings the same as you. I don't want anything from you after the fact, and I certainly am not demanding that you marry me because of it." As she turned her head to meet his gaze, there was nothing but amusement in her eyes. "I merely want to spend time with you, no matter the capacity."

"That is quite how I feel as well." He kept to the pavement that went around the square so she wouldn't need to walk through mud, but this was the perfect opportunity to delve more into her life. "Since meeting you, I have admired how you work and how your mind puts things together; however, beyond that, I am in the dark on what kind of woman you are. I would like to change that."

Would that sound too much like a declaration or an indication of courtship? Did it matter?

Slowly, Cate nodded. "I have no issue with that. What would you like to know?"

What, indeed? "Uh…" Suddenly, his mind went blank, then he cleared his throat. "What is your favorite dessert?"

"Raspberry trifle." She slid a glance to him. "Yours?"

"Sweet mince pies. Mrs. Travers makes them at this time of year only, and I can hardly have enough of them. Would make myself sick on them if I could."

The sound of her laughter went through him and lit tiny fires in his blood. "I could see how you might find yourself addicted." She held her umbrella a little higher. "There is a special sort of gingerbread cake my grandmother used to have made just for Christmas dinner. I haven't had it since she died, and hadn't realized how much I missed it until now."

Barr tucked that information away. Perhaps if he could meet with Mrs. Travers and talk to her about it, she might be able to find a recipe similar enough to bake the cake for his own Christmas dinner… that he would invite Cate and her father to. "What color do you favor when you have gowns and dresses made?"

"Oh, blue or green." She shrugged and a slow smile curved her lips. "I often dream that, if I were independently wealthy and my father ever took me to a society event that was elegant enough, that I would have a gown made in silver." Another laugh escaped her. "As it is, most of my clothing is designed for research in mind. Books and shelves are dusty. Crawling and climbing to reach tucked away volumes or going through forgotten places is a messy business, so I wear simple cuts and drab colors that would hold up well to laundering."

"Ah, and now I have another piece of the puzzle." His mind fairly percolated, for he had an inkling of what he might wish to secure her as a present for Christmas. "What is your opinion on the Regent?"

She snorted. "Don't you dare think to drag me into a political discussion. However, I think he uses government resources in a wasteful way, and he is far too careless and practices excess in every aspect of his life." Then she winked at him. "Let's leave it at that."

"Very well." Barr nodded, but he was having the best time.

"If you could only travel to one country, which one would it be and why?"

"You certainly know how to ask difficult questions, don't you?"

He turned them around on the pavement to start the walk back toward his townhouse. "It's the easiest and quickest way to gain knowledge."

"No doubt you would probably assume I'd say Egypt, since that is the most popular choice of explorers and budding tomb robbers, but there is a large part of me that wishes to go to Rome. Can you imagine what lies beneath those streets and in the catacombs?"

"Besides long dead bodies?"

"Well, yes, of course, and treasures of all kinds." She shrugged but the light in her eyes was unmistakable. "Or to see the lovely countrysides of that peninsula? The vineyards? Feel the sun on my face… if it ever does return after this abysmal time. And I could overcome the sickness from the sea. Beyond that? Again, if coin wasn't an issue, I'm not certain where I would go. Perhaps America, to see if they are as savage as the king wished for everyone to believe?"

"Ha! And if that land is uncivilized?"

"Then I should just go on to somewhere else. India might be so interesting, even if it's half a world away and would take seemingly an eternity to arrive there."

"It would be lovely to have all the time in the world to go wherever the wind took us and see more of the world than is contained in England." With a sigh, he frowned. "And be out of the damned rain."

"You certainly have no fondness for such precipitation," she mentioned, with amusement in her voice.

"Of course, living in England, one needs to expect and become accustomed to such wretched weather, but I would enjoy a few days a week—perhaps a month if that's all I were to be allotted—where the sun would shine and I wouldn't need to slog my way through a day." Did it make him seem demented? "In any event, I'm sure eventually everything will come right again. Until then, I can dream."

"Those are always free and plentiful." She laid a gloved hand on his arm. "Why did you not travel with your wife and children? From all I know of you, it would have been the perfect educational tool for them. And you are a duke, so nothing would be out of your reach."

"I don't know about that." He peered at her as best he could with the umbrellas and the brim of her bonnet. "I had responsibilities and social obligations. My son was away at school, and my daughter had her tutors here. My wife was deeply involved with her charities and causes. I didn't wish to disrupt any of that, and by the time the children were old enough to enjoy traveling, my wife perished."

"I'm sorry to bring up such painful memories."

"It is not just you; it is this time of year." When she nodded, no doubt remembering her mother, he huffed out a breath. "My wife and I were the typical couple of the *beau monde*. We conducted our lives much as we were expected, as we'd both been raised, for she was the daughter of an earl."

"So then you had very little freedom to explore the man you might have been if you didn't have expectations of you." Sadness reflected in her expression. "That must have been difficult."

"While that's true to an extent, I grew used to it, but truth to tell, I don't want my children to feel those pressures."

"They will, though, merely because they are children of a duke." When she dropped her hand from his arm, he mourned the loss of her warmth. "But you can at least encourage them and teach them to have balance in their lives, so they don't feel trapped."

He nodded. "That is exactly it, and I have told them both the same. Yes, they do have certain responsibilities—I'm a firm believer that those of us with privilege need to give back to the society who placed us here—but I want them to be happy as well.

I want them to know there is more to their existence than the gilded cage of society."

"You are a good man, Barr. I know they adore you as a father."

"I appreciate that." His townhouse came into sight, and that was a bit depressing, for it meant his walk with her was nearly concluded. "Above all of that, without the children here, it *is* a tad lonely. One of the things I adored with my wife was her companionship. It was lovely having someone to share all the little things with, the quiet times, to have someone beside me, lying in bed and talking about our day those nights we shared a suite."

"You might not believe it, but you are quite adorable. I hope you find that again with someone, for I don't think you are the type of man to remain alone."

"Indeed." Then, after they'd gained the gardens at the back of his townhouse again, he brought them to a halt, gently cupped her cheek, and as he tilted her head back a touch, he brought his lips to hers. There would hardly be witnesses, since they were much alone on this Sunday afternoon, and there was something so intimate and cozy about showing affection for this woman in the rain. And what was more, he had a feeling that what he was beginning to feel for her went far beyond the heat and passion of having carnal needs met. When he pulled back, he offered her a faint smile. "Thank you for spending the afternoon with me. While you return to your translation efforts, I can make you some tea and forage for sweets in the kitchen."

"I would find that perfectly acceptable." As she made her way toward the library doors, he followed. "Tomorrow, I am not scheduled at the lending library, but I do need to pop into the shops. Unfortunately, I'm realizing too late that time is running out before Christmas. I promise, though, that I'll work additional hours on the translation."

He nodded as they entered the house. "You needn't finish it before that day, you know. There is time enough afterward if you'd like to spend that time with your father." Though he would miss her presence.

"Fear not, Scarborough. Papa is lost enough in his research; he'll hardly remember there is a holiday unless I physically tug him from his chair."

"I see." But relief twisted down his spine, for it was one more day he would spend with her. What would Travers say about that?

CHAPTER THIRTEEN

December 23, 1816

"I THINK I need to take a break or else my eyes will cross." So saying, Cate planted her elbows on the desktop in the study and rubbed her eyes with her fingers. Her back ached as well, for sitting at weird angles to make the best use of the candlelight had cramped her muscles. Then she yawned, for she'd been working on the translation for the better part of four hours.

Of course, she was talking to herself because the duke had worked on renovations while she'd been busy and unaware of the world around her, but now she only had perhaps the last third of the book to translate. Some of the words and phrases had eluded her, so she'd had to guess at what the author had meant, and some pages were damaged. In those places, there was not enough text to piece together the narrative, but it didn't matter. The story as it was coming together was concerning and quite maudlin.

Needing movement and to work out the knots from her muscles, Cate stood up from the chair. She wandered over to the window where the steady drum of rain beat against the glass. The floorplan of the duke's townhouse was lovely, for the building rested on a corner lot, which allowed many of the rooms on the south side to have access to windows. In fact, unless the rooms were interior, there were windows on three sides of the town-house. Whenever the sun *did* return, that natural light would be most welcome.

Of course, she would have finished the translation by then and would have no cause to enjoy such a thing. To say nothing to the fact that her association with Scarborough would undoubtedly end. What exactly were they to each other? Lovers? Convenient trysting partners? If he asked, would she agree to become his mistress knowing there was every possibility that we might marry someone else for love and that she would need to stand on the sidelines watching that story unfold?

No thank you. I have more respect for myself than all that.

The sad thing about this was he hadn't spoken of his feelings for her—if he indeed had any over and above lust and desire—but to be fair, she hadn't either. How could she when she couldn't puzzle it out for herself? Of course, she had to remain realistic about her position. It didn't matter if she did have feelings for him. He was a duke; she was the spinster daughter of a Cambridge professor, only here to provide translation services. Outside of the carnal exercise they shared, there wasn't much else between them.

Was there? And perhaps more to the point, did she want there to be? For all her insistence that she wouldn't marry unless love was present, what if she *did* fall for the duke, but he had no intention of asking her for anything beyond what they had now, especially once the translation had concluded?

Gah! Why is doing anything with a man so complicated?

"Ah, Cate, it is good to see that you've managed to tear yourself away from the book." As the duke strode into the study, he offered her the particular grin she suspected he reserved only for her, but why? Why would he do such a thing? Or was he not aware of it? "How goes the translation? When I last checked in, you were fully engaged and didn't even know I was there."

She turned away from the window, but that was a mistake, for her gaze landed fully on him, and dear heavens, he was quite handsome in the dim illumination and weak light from the overcast late afternoon. The silver that glinted through his black hair made her want to throw caution to the wind and run her fingers through those tresses, but it was the hint of an evening shadow that clung to his jaw and chin that had her knees wobbling. Such a feature on a man was one of her favorite things. What would that bit of roughness feel like rasping against her thighs?

Making an effort to shove the naughty thoughts away, she offered him a smile that she feared was a miserable business. "It has been quite intense, but I have another third of the book to go. It might, indeed, be finished by Christmas." Another depressing thought, for she would probably not see him after that day.

A frown tugged at the corners of his sensual mouth. "You seem a bit out of sorts. Is all well?"

"Oh, yes, of course." It was then that she realized he'd removed his jacket, cuffs, collar, cravat, and waistcoat at some point in the afternoon, and that the sleeves of his shirt had been rolled to his elbows. No doubt it was easier to maneuver when papering walls when his arms weren't restricted. And he was mouthwatering. "I was just thinking about the bit I've translated today." It was easier than telling him that his presence confused her as much as it aroused. "Would you like to hear the part of the story I uncovered?"

"Of course. I have been patiently waiting for the next installment."

Drat him, but that grin would be the death of her if she wasn't careful. She nodded as she drifted back toward the desk where she'd left her notes. "Well, there's no doubt the story is becoming exciting now. The pharaoh's son thinks there is an unloyal servant in the palace."

"Oh? Who?"

She knew the intrigue of the tale would grip him. "I wasn't able to discern a name, but apparently this man wanted the pharaoh's son's lover for himself. He wasn't happy that she'd chosen the son over him."

"Did they previously know each other?"

"That is another thing I wasn't able to find any information about. It could have been mentioned throughout the water damaged section, but the author wasn't keen on mentioning names, as far as I can tell." Cate consulted her notes. "In any event, our hero witnessed this man speaking with one of the pharaoh's advisors, but he was across a courtyard and too far away to overhear. There is no doubt he is worried."

"I can just imagine. He probably wishes to make plans in order to remove his lover from the palace and bring her away, so she'll be safe."

"Yes, exactly." Cate nodded. "The story has taken quite a maudlin turn, which has also made translation difficult."

For long moments, silence reigned between them.

"Well, I hope they are successful in their plans to flee."

"So do I, but from what I can tell, it's not looking favorable."

"Damn, I'd hoped they might have lived happily ever after."

She couldn't help but sigh. When they'd talked in the rain yesterday and he shared some of what his marriage had been like, she assumed if he wished to marry again, he would choose a woman from the *ton* who had much in common with him. If she were honest with herself, it was always highly unlikely that a woman like her could ever hope for anything with him over and above what they shared physically. After all, their relationship hadn't been based on anything except mutual attraction and need. There was nothing wrong with that, but part of her wished there might be room for more.

"There is no evidence as of yet that they didn't. Perhaps we should wait for the end of the tale." When she met his gaze, his was unreadable, the emotions hidden.

He glanced at her with a frown. "You and I both know they didn't have a future together since they were from two different worlds. As the son of a pharaoh, he would have had responsibilities he couldn't ignore."

"Oh, I'm well aware of that." Her thoughts went immediately to Scarborough. Did he still labor under such for himself? Did he want more of the same now, or would he choose freedom and adventure of responsibility? "In my heart of hearts, I'd like to hope it didn't matter to them. As he wrote, love is love." Oddly, her chin trembled before she could control her emotions. "I'd like to think love was bigger than any obstacles they faced."

"So would I." The duke moved across the room toward the door. When she assumed he'd leave her to the translations again, he paused. "It's growing late in the evening. Dinner is soon. I'd thought you would have gone home to your father by now."

"Oh, he plans to have dinner with some friends at one of his favorite pubs." She stacked her notebook, the original book, and her notes into a neat pile. "I shall take a tray in my room later tonight since I don't have much of an appetite just now."

"No need." He nodded and his expression was both cheeky and mysterious. "You can have dinner with me. I believe Mrs. Travers has set it without the hour." Yet when he closed the door and turned the locking mechanism, it was her turn to frown.

What was he about? "I suppose I could do that. I do enjoy Mrs. Travers' cooking, yet..." She really shouldn't. It was merely an added temptation, and they had both courted enough scandal over the past week.

"Then it's settled." As he spoke, Barr closed the distance between them. He paused in front of her with a certain hunger in his eyes that immediately fired her own. "We can discuss topics of the day, and it will be a lovely change from what I'm used to— eating alone with either a newspaper or a book."

"Perhaps you should think about inviting over some of your neighbors to keep you company."

"Most are away from London at this time of year." When he cupped her cheek, Cate couldn't help but nuzzle into his palm. "While I'll admit, it's slightly lonely, I'll wager you feel the same, but you are too strong-willed to show it."

"Perhaps." What was more, she'd no idea that subject had been weighing so heavily upon her shoulders. "Papa is always busy, weather it is with his research and paper writing, his own friends, or his work at Cambridge." The touch of Barr's fingers over her skin as he slowly drew his hand down to her neck threatened to see her undone. "For a long time, I pursued my own interests since my mother died, and that distracted me for a while. But I suppose my ill-advised relationships with previous employers was only an extension of grief and loneliness." Why was she telling him this? And why the deuce was her throat tight as if she wanted to cry? "It has never been more obvious to me that I should have chased marriage when I had the chance."

Would showing such vulnerability trigger pity from him? That was certainly not what she wanted.

"Sometimes, when we don't know how to grieve, we convince ourselves we don't have the time or that we just don't feel things that deeply." The rumble of his voice brought both comfort and need. "But you can't keep postponing it. Trust me, I know, for I fell apart a couple of years after my wife died." His fingers at her nape gently urged her closer to his body. "Perhaps that was why you pursued men all wrong for you, as a way to release those pent-up emotions."

It was startling in its simplicity, and she widened her eyes. "What if I'm still doing it by being here with you?"

"Only you can know for certain, but I would like to think there is a genuine connection between us, for knowing we're each using the other for our own personal urges is rather a messy business." He slid the pad of his thumb over her trembling bottom lip. "Truth be told? I don't believe you are that sort of woman."

"And neither are you that sort of man," she responded in a barely-there whisper. "How will I know the reason?"

"You shall either feel happiness after all is said and done, or you will still have an empty pit in your belly."

She swallowed hard and nodded. "Is that what happened with you?"

"More or less. Thankfully, I had my children and my staff around me to help guide me back into the light. Then I found fulfillment in my renovations, but even then, I half suspect that is still a form of hiding."

"Yet you seem to be waiting for something, for someone, perhaps permission to take up the reins of your life again. Why?"

"I don't know." The duke shook his head, but that hunger in his eyes didn't dim. His gaze dropped to her mouth. "I'd like to think that the answer will reveal itself to me as soon as that piece of the puzzle is found."

Was she that piece? Did he want her to be? Cate rested a palm on his chest, felt the race of his heartbeat beneath her fingertips. "What do we do in the meantime?" She deliberately left the statement open to interpretation, for she wanted him to definitively tell her that he wanted her… for more than a source of repletion.

Because I think I might be falling for you…

"Ah, Cate…" With a soft growl, Barrington crushed his lips to hers in a savage kiss that told her in no uncertain terms he wanted her and the momentary mess she represented. By the time they wrenched apart, they were both breathless. He sought her gaze with his. "What is this hold you have on me?"

"Whatever it is, I'm caught up in it too." Needing to touch him, she tugged his shirttail from his trousers and then shoved her hands beneath his shirt. The heat of him seared her fingertips, lit fires in her blood. Her body fairly hummed with need and was fueled by the stark want in his sapphire eyes. "Don't make me regret showing you how close to vulnerability I apparently am."

It was folly to give in. Surely, a mistake to couple with him again. Yet breaking away from his embrace was like trying to pin a cloud.

"Emotions are not a death knell, especially with someone who understands."

"Careful, Your Grace. That charm will land you into trouble."

Or her since they'd not been careful in any of their couplings. A shiver went down her spine when he kissed her once more, kissed her hard so there were no doubts of how much he desired her. Over and over, he devoured her mouth as if she'd be instantly ripped from his life. She gave as good as she got, for she'd never been afraid of going after what she wanted in life, and soon they were panting, hands searching, fingers trailing over familiar skin, lost to the heat between them.

And oh, how she wanted this to last!

As desire overrode common sense, he wrenched his mouth from hers. "Where?"

The choices were varied and interesting. "The desk is most logical."

"Hardly out of the erotic book."

"If they'd had desks, I'm sure it would have been." She squealed when he picked her up then carried her to the desk and deposited her arse upon it. Books and papers tumbled to the floor with flutters and thuds.

She tugged him closer. "How is it that you make me forget everything else in an instant? And at my age?"

"As if you are ancient." His chuckle tickled through her chest. "You are the perfect age." Then, with a grin, the duke settled between her naturally splayed legs. He put a hand at her back and proceeded to pleasure her breasts, sucking the rigid nubs of her nipples through the fabric of her dress.

"Oh, mercy…" Her soft cries of enjoyment sounded overly loud in the quiet of the room. Instinctively, she knew this coupling would be frantic and fast, but she didn't care, for she was nearly out of her mind with need. By the time she reached for his front falls, his length was engorged and wonderfully hard. As his thick member sprang from his breeches, he paused long enough to flick his gaze over her form. Appreciation was evident in his eyes.

"Why do you look at me like that?"

"Do you have any idea how lovely you are? How every man in London who passed on courting you are idiots of the first order?"

"Oh!" Her heart squeezed with an overabundance of emotion. "Such gammon."

"Hardly, and in fact, I…" At the last second, he bit off whatever he'd been about to say, but she didn't mind. It meant he might be thinking about the future.

With her in it.

"I rather doubt this coupling will go slowly. I've thought of nothing else this whole afternoon than ravishing you." Before she could respond, the duke shoved up yards of her skirting, and when she was bared to his gaze, he gripped her hips and brought her forward until she balanced on the edge of the desk. "You are much like a rare book I want to horde all to myself."

"Waxing poetic tonight, Scarborough," she managed to gasp, but then he claimed her lips once more, and her ability to think was swept away on a hot tide of passion.

Shortly after, Barr found her center with the tip of his member, then thrust swiftly in until he was fully seated in her passage. "Oh, God," he whispered against her lips. "Always amazing."

"I quite concur." Cate clutched at his forearms as she moaned. Need mirrored in his eyes. "Don't hold back. Give me all of you… give me the man you wish to be."

He nodded. "That feels right." His thrusts were frantic, hard, and deep. At one point, he paused to hold her gaze, but she wanted none of that. Cate held his head between her hands, brought his forehead to hers, and kissed him like a woman desperate for the very air he breathed. Perhaps she was; it was difficult to tell anymore. The duke kissed her back. Never had the connection between them been so strong.

Did he feel it too? Would he eventually want something beyond the physical?

Then, he straightened as urgency drove his actions. He held her hips, the outside of her thighs in an effort to apparently go as deep as he could, stroking again and again into her while she held onto his arms and canted her hips to meet his thrusts.

Heat and pressure stacked low in her belly. Pleasure rushed through her core, but Barr's strokes grew quicker and faster. When she broke with a cry upon her lips and tears in her eyes, tumbling over that glorious edge into bliss, he kissed her, taking most of the sound into himself as he came with her. They shattered together, and it was one of the most intimately erotic things she'd ever experienced, for this joining was different. When she opened her eyes and sought out his gaze, he grinned and ground his pelvis into hers.

"Woman, you wear me out in the best of ways. I've never had that in my life before." Swiftly, he kissed her. "Hell, I've never been this man before either, so thank you for that."

"I had nothing to do with it. You would have found your way eventually with a different lady." Her limbs shook as she clung to him. "But I understand the sentiment."

"Don't discount what you've brought here." With a slight frown, Barr removed them both to one of the leather, winged-back chairs. After he sank into, he cradled her on his lap, her legs on either side of him.

"At this rate, that book might not get translated until the new year." As her heartbeat calmed and she slumped against him with her arms loosely looped about his shoulders, Cate was certain what she felt for the duke went far beyond lust and passion. Stupidly, she'd given him her heart, as she'd done twice before when she'd had carnal relationships with her previous employers.

Would this one end in disaster as well? Absolutely, he wouldn't make her an offer other than that of a mistress. And neither should he. Barr was a duke. She was… nothing special when seen by society's eyes.

"I won't complain if you don't." As he nuzzled his lips into the crook of her shoulder, he slipped his hands to the small of her back. "I guess we've worked up an appetite for dinner."

"So it would seem, and let us hope none of your staff heard what we just did." They couldn't continue in this vein. It simply wasn't sustainable, for that passion would eventually fade.

Wouldn't it?

He snorted with laughter. "Well, my valet is *quite* nosy." But he wasn't apparently in a hurry to release her. "In all honesty, though, we should probably make ourselves presentable. My butler will no doubt come looking for me, and I need to remember where I left the other half of my clothing."

Which reminded her, she'd still yet to see him naked. "And I should tidy up this room." After kissing his lips, Cate slipped from his lap. "Christmas Eve is tomorrow. The lending library is closed, but I need to drop by a few shops before coming over here. Unless you don't wish for me to work on the translation." Thank goodness her dress was a navy wool blend, for the wet marks from where he'd pleasured her nipples weren't immediately noticeable, but the remembrance of that sent heat into her cheeks.

"No, absolutely come by. The staff likes to make the day a gay affair." As he set his clothing to rights, he regarded her. "And honestly, I would like to share that with you. Invite your father to dinner tomorrow night. I don't want him alone."

Another piece of her heart flew into his keeping. "I will. Thank you."

What am I going to do now?

CHAPTER FOURTEEN

December 24, 1816
Christmas Eve

ANTICIPATION AND EXCITEMENT buzzed at the base of Barr's spine as he rapped on the door frame of the study so he wouldn't startle Cate while she worked. If he allowed himself, he'd become caught up in the recollection of what they'd shared together in this very room. That moment of vulnerability she'd let him see had been everything, and had made her even more approachable. To say nothing of how that quick, frantic coupling had bonded them even closer.

What the devil should I do about that?

"Might I interrupt you for a moment?"

She glanced at him from behind the desk. "Of course." When she offered him a soft smile, his world tilted, and a queer little hitch went through his heart. "Is there something pressing?"

"Not at all." As he came into the room, he glanced at the window. "The rain has slacked off somewhat, and from what I can see, there is a brief break in the clouds, so I'd like to make the best use of the reprieve from the precipitation."

"What have you planned? It is Christmas Eve, so I rather doubt the shops will be open. Perhaps the poulteress or a bakery? But you would push your luck to try."

"I am not interested in any of that." He rested his gaze upon her. Had she always been so uncommonly beautiful? In the flickering candlelight, he discerned tiny golden flecks in the brown depths of her irises, and why had he never seen the small dark beauty mark over her right eyebrow or the slight dimple in her left cheek when she smiled?

Because you've allowed your prick to lead you this whole time.

Perhaps his conscience was correct, and that needed to change. He cleared his throat. "I was thinking of driving out to Hyde Park for a quick visit."

A frown tugged the corners of her kissable mouth downward. "Whyever for?"

Heat crept up the back of his neck. "I would like to bring back some mistletoe."

Surprise flickered through her expression. "Mistletoe?"

Barr nodded. "As I told you before, my wife was insistent that the holiday was marked with sprigs of the plant, and in years past, my son went out to Hyde Park and fetched some, but since he's not here, I thought I'd do it, and I'd hoped you might like to accompany me merely to get out of the house for a bit."

Would she think him too lost in the past or in silly traditions that had no bearing now?

With a glance to the window, she nodded. "I would be game for an outing."

"Excellent. Shall we crack on, then? Hyde Park is the most likely place we'll begin, though I have heard stories that sometimes mistletoe has been found in apple trees in the countryside. If not, we'll search in one of the other parks." He shrugged. "Once we're sufficiently chilled and have the plant in hand, we'll return here for some much-needed tea." It was ridiculous to be so excited for an outing in the drizzle, wasn't it?

A half hour later saw them in a closed carriage. A footman rode beside the driver—it seemed the young man was only too eager to escape the house as well—and instead of the drizzle of before, the temperatures had dropped, which led to snow flurries.

"I am looking forward to that tea later," Cate mentioned as she gave into a shiver from where she sat on the bench opposite him. "Just the other day, I'd wondered if London would experience snow like the northern part of the country is having currently, and now I know."

It was insanity how wildly the weather swung. "At least it's a change from the rain." Yet would all the puddles and rutting in the roads freeze and make travel even more hazardous? It was anyone's guess, but despite the fact a holiday was tomorrow, there was much vehicle and pedestrian traffic all through Mayfair.

"There is that." She offered a smile but then turned her face to look out the window. The brim of her bonnet shielded her eyes from his view. "A part of me hopes London will be covered with snow by tomorrow even though it will make a mess of things." Pressing a gloved fingertip to the window glass, she sighed. "But it's so pretty, almost romantic in its simplicity."

It was another insight into the woman she was, and the realization that she wasn't complicated gave him a feeling of peace. Nothing about her demanded anything from him except his attention and notice. She never hinted for gifts, or the use of his box at the opera, and never once did she accuse him of inappropriate conduct or want him to marry her. That added to her intelligence, her compassion, her zest for learning all had his admiration for her rising.

"The snow almost gives the world a fresh start with the blanket of white."

"It does." When Cate rested her gaze back on him, she smiled. "The winter is just so cozy. I adore sitting near a fire when flakes are coming down outside." A throaty sort of sound escaped her as she laughed. "When I was a young girl, sometimes Papa would take Mama and I out to the country. We would rent a cottage and spend a couple of weeks tramping through the snow and sometimes sledding. Papa was never much for hunting, but he is an avid bird watcher. Fills countless pages of notebooks with jottings about the birds he's seen, how they behave, and the like." She shrugged. "He's a dear, of course, but his love of birds has been replaced with Roman antiquities and history, I think."

"It is good to have pursues and hobbies that fill us with interests."

"Do you have any besides doing renovations with your own two hands?"

"Well, I have always thought it might be lovely to learn how to sail. Since my country estate is very near to Cornwall and the sea, I'm curious about taking a boat out and tacking the waves."

"Oh!" Her eyes lit. "I think you would be a fine sailor indeed."

Barr couldn't help but chuckle. "I'd imagine a few dunks in the sea would knock that notion out of my mind."

"You'll never know until you try it."

"Yet you couldn't come since the sea makes you ill."

She shrugged. "Surely, there must be a cure."

Suddenly, he could imagine next summertime with the sun shining down to reflect on the water. There was laughter in the air as well as the cry of gulls and other water birds, but Cate was there as well. She walked along the shore with her brown hair unbound and tossed on the breeze, but what was more, his children were there, talking and joking with her, and he could almost feel how her hand felt in his.

Did he have the courage to make that a reality or was it merely wishful thinking? What he truly needed was to talk again with Travers or perhaps his cook. He needed advice from the people who knew him the best, or perhaps he'd write a letter to his son. That was overdue, in any event.

By the time the carriage arrived at Hyde Park, the flurries were coming down in earnest, and the flakes were big and fluffy, much like pieces of lace.

Once he alighted and then assisted Cate out, he addressed the young footman, whose name was Ronald. "The mission today is to procure a few sprigs of mistletoe. Since it's a bit like a thief and lives off healthy trees, we'll no doubt find it in branches of oak trees and the like. The snow might make climbing a bit challenging, but we'll manage."

The footman nodded. "I've brought along a saw, Your Grace, as well as a knife."

"Good man." Barr glanced at Cate. "Ready?"

"I suppose so. It's been ages since I hunted for any sort of holiday greenery." She laid a hand on his arm, and he rather enjoyed that bit of connection.

"Then we'll have a bit of an adventure." He escorted her along behind the footman. "Did your parents ever put much stock in the power of mistletoe?"

"Ha." She chuckled and amusement reflected in her eyes. "Not a bit of it. My father often called the plant a parasite, for that is what it is, and he never failed to remind everyone that the plant is quite toxic. My mother was forever planning her next social engagement, so she let him ramble on, but I rather doubt she even knew what he talked about. They adored each other, of course, yet their interests rarely put them together beyond the domestic."

"I'll wager you take after your father?"

"Perhaps, since I find myself gravitating toward bookish things over societal ones."

"There is nothing wrong with that."

"I wonder sometimes." But she said nothing else as they walked deeper into the park.

A good half hour passed as the three of them browsed beneath countless trees in the hunt of mistletoe. Every once in a while, Cate put out a hand to catch snowflakes on her glove, and the delight in her expression tugged at his heart.

Then a shout from Ronald brought him beneath a particularly large oak tree, whose dried brown leaves still clung to some of its branches despite the winter season having just started.

"I think I see some," the footman said as he pointed through the branches halfway up into the tree. "Barely visible, but it's just there."

With a frown, Barr took a peek where the footman indicated. There was the hint of white berries in what appeared to be a rounded wad of yellowish green leaves. "Fair enough. You climb first and I'll follow behind."

Surprise once more went through Cate's expression. "You intend to go up into that tree?"

"Yes, why not? How can I expect Ronald to risk his life if I'm not willing to do the same?" One of his eyebrows rose. "Besides, I used to do the same all the time when I was a youth. It should be easy work."

"Except you're not a youth any longer, and that was a long time ago."

Another blow to his ego, but he brushed it aside. "You'll see. Don't fret. All will be well." Then he nodded at the footman. "Lead on, Ronald."

"Oh, please be careful, the both of you." She huffed. "I can't really see that a bit of plant life is worth the risk."

"It is, you'll see." Barr couldn't help but wink at her. Truly, he couldn't explain the urge to have the damned mistletoe other than it was one of his wife's favorite traditions, and that he wanted to share it with Cate. And if he were honest with himself, he wanted the freedom to be able to kiss her without having to do it in private. "Onward, Ronald!"

He didn't quite count on the fact that the daily rain and damp coupled with the snow and the cold would make climbing a tree a bit more difficult than he'd assumed, but he did his best. Ronald scampered up far more quickly than Barr climbed.

As the footman reached a stout branch and scooted on his arse toward where the mistletoe rested, when Barr was halfway up the damned tree, he lost his footing, and though he scrambled for purchase with his boots, he wasn't quite fast enough to find a handhold either.

"Argh!" The trip down to the ground was accomplished with haste since he fell from the tree. As Cate uttered a half-stifled scream of alarm, he landed hard on his back, which knocked the wind from his lungs for several moments.

"Scarborough!" She ran to his location and then threw herself onto her knees by his side. "Are you all right? Are you in pain?"

He could only wheeze in response, for it was impossible to draw a breath or even speak.

"Damn you, Barr." She frowned as she stared down at him with a mixture of concern and horror in her eyes. "Say something." Apparently not wanting to wait, Cate slid her hands over his limbs, his ribcage, seemingly everywhere. "I don't feel broken bones. Perhaps you cracked open your head after this stunt, but I fear your skull is far too thick and stubborn."

Finally, he could take in enough air to his lungs to grunt. He cleared his throat while batting away her hands. "Leave off." After sucking in another breath, he coughed. "I'm well enough. Just embarrassed." As proof, he moved his arms and legs, then his head and made sure his spine wasn't broken. "I don't understand how my foot slipped. Could have sworn I was steady." When he stared up at her, his heart squeezed at the fleeting fear that went through her expression. "Sorry to worry you."

"Perhaps it is the—"

"Don't you dare say it's the damned curse," he interrupted in a breathless way but couldn't help but laugh with her in both relief and hilarity.

A grudging grin curved her lips. "Well, I'll just think it then." She shook her head. "That was quite a risk. You should know better than that."

Oddly enough, it was lovely knowing someone cared enough about him to scold him for doing something stupid. "I should, of course, but I was trying to impress you. Clearly, though, I'm not as young as I used to be."

She sputtered. "It's not that, it's just—"

"Hush, Miss Pickwick," Barr murmured as he looked up at her. Then, because he was perhaps cheeky and he didn't much care what anyone thought, he hooked a gloved hand around her nape and brought her down where he claimed her lips in a kiss despite the footman still in the tree.

"Oh!" Her eyes opened wide in surprise from the sweet gesture, and he lingered there for a few seconds before pulling away. A shuddering sigh left her throat. "Why did you do that?"

"It's obvious." Barr pointed upward at the footman who laughed as he freed a big wad of mistletoe from the branch. "We are very clearly under the mistletoe, Miss Pickwick."

"There are times when I don't know what to make of you, Scarborough." But Cate laughed, and her smile reflected in her eyes. In that moment, when she was obviously relieved that he hadn't injured himself, she was easily the most beautiful woman he'd seen in quite a while. "So I'll just do this." Leaning over him, she fit her lips to his and then kissed him back.

Christ, but it would be all too easy to take command of the embrace, to continue you it until heat consumed them both, but kept a tight hold on his control, releasing her almost immediately. "Let me up, unless it's your intention to leave me frozen to the ground?"

"It's what you deserve, but I don't want you catching a head cold." But she assisted him to his feet, and then stood close to him as if she didn't quite trust him not to suffer a collapse.

Barr waved a hand at the footman as the mistletoe fell from the branch as it was freed. "I think we'll only require this one bunch. It's large enough that we can divide it if necessary. Come on down, Ronald. You did well."

"Thank you, Your Grace. It was my pleasure."

By the time they returned to the carriage, and it lurched forward to begin the trip home, Barr was satisfied with the outing. The mistletoe rested on the bench beside him, and he grinned as he sought out Cate's gaze across the narrow aisle.

"Are you certain you haven't suffered from the fall out of the tree?"

"Yes, yes, I'm quite all right. I'll have bruises on the morrow, but otherwise, my ego hurts more than anything else." He sobered. "Again, I'm sorry to have worried you."

"I'm sorry as well. I have no right to take offense when you do something stupid." She glanced out the window, perhaps to avoid his gaze. "Do you want to know about the bit of the story I managed to translate today before you dragged me out into the snow?"

Which was falling with a bit more energy so that it stuck to the ground, the streets, and the rooftops. "Yes, please."

"Very well." With a nod, Cate returned her attention to him. "It seems the pharaoh's son arranged to spirit away his lover from the palace on a dark, moonless night. According to the text, there were rumors that his father would order her killed at first light, so he had to act fast."

"How terrible, and all on the advice of his son's rival? Where is the due process?"

She snorted. "Despot rulers and people with ultimate power like a pharaoh don't care about investigations. They want to make a show, make an example, of anyone they feel will oppose them or make people think differently."

"Perhaps." Barr nodded, and could think of at least two examples from the world in which they lived.

"Anyway, the young man had her dress in black robes, wear a wig so she wouldn't immediately be discovered. Then he took his lover to the river where they'd met numerous times before."

"There is something quite melancholy in that."

"Oh, yes." Cate nodded. "At the river, in their special place, they had intercourse one last time on the soft grass that grew on the banks amidst the reeds. The night was even more special, for they also exchanged their love for each other through words, even though it was forbidden. It mattered not them."

"At least there was that." Yet Barr was caught up in the tale. "What happened next?"

She shrugged. "He put her in a boat with all sorts of treasures, food, clothes, and other supplies, assured her that he would meet her somewhere down river as soon as he could get away. According to the text, he told the boatman to look after her because she was the keeper of his heart, and paid the boatman handsomely to secure the journey."

Barr frowned. "And she was gone."

"Yes. It seems so."

"Well damn. Is that the end of the book?"

"No, there are still a handful of pages needing translation. And I could even be wrong in what I've already done due to the damaged pages and smeared ink."

"I rather doubt that. You are one of the most capable women I have ever met." Leaning forward, he laid a hand on her knee. The reaction snapping between them was immediate and heated. "Promise me that you won't work on the translation until after Boxing Day. Enjoy your holiday, but remember to escort your father here tonight for dinner and parlor games. I don't wish for him to be forgotten either."

"I will. Thank you for the generosity." Her smile lit him up from the inside out. "I know he will have a lovely time, as will I."

"Good. I'm looking forward to it." Though he suspected one evening acting as a family wouldn't be nearly enough with her.

Was there a future between them? Was there anything else between them when the heat was removed? The remembrance of the concern in her eyes when he'd fallen out of the tree was uppermost in his mind. A woman who only wanted a man for his body wouldn't have looked at him like that.

Perhaps there was hope after all, and damn if he would let their story end like that poor Egyptian couple from thousands of years ago.

CHAPTER FIFTEEN

Later that night

CATE ALLOWED HERSELF a soft smile as she watched the antics of Barr, her father, and many of the servants while they played a game of charades.

Everyone had assembled in the drawing room following dinner where Mrs. Travers had outdone herself with the offerings. The dinner was so lovely, Cate could hardly wait to see what would happen tomorrow night on Christmas proper. Despite the shortages and scarcities in securing supplies for the meal, the staff had done a miraculous job of it, and because of those things, the staff ate with the duke and his guests.

No one took issue with that, and it was rather a wonderful concept not being separated due to class differences.

Like a family.

As the men good-naturedly competed against each other, Cate returned her gaze to the duke. It should be criminal for a man to look so handsome, and the fact that Barr did that without trying only made him that much better. Of course, Travers had something to do with it too, for he'd no doubt chosen the clothing. Tonight, Barr wore dark gray breeches with highly polished boots. He'd paired it with a charcoal superfine jacket and a waistcoat of gold brocade. The snowy folds of his cravat drew her attention to his rugged jawline.

Good heavens, how much did she want to press her lips to

the skin beneath that jaw, that chin, to feel the difference between smooth and rough?

Put him out of your mind, Catherine. Hasn't your existence already been confusing enough?

With that at the forefront, she glanced away and then drifted to a knot of the women comprised of the housekeeper, Mrs. Travers the cook, and several of the maids. "We should, at least, get up some juicy gossip while the men are distracted," she said as she joined the cook on a low sofa.

Mrs. Travers chuckled. She smiled as her husband managed to stump Barr's team and win the current round. "I'm afraid I haven't been aware of anything untoward, since I've either been here or in our own residence." One of her eyebrows went up, though, and she lowered her voice as shouts from the men echoed through the room. "However, the only potential scandal I can think of is your interesting relationship with His Grace."

Oh, dear.

Cate glanced at the duke. He happened to meet her gaze, and he shot her a grin before it was his turn to enact whatever the clue was for his team. "I'm just here to translate his Egyptian book of prose."

"I wonder if that is true." Mrs. Travers scooted a bit closer to her on the sofa. "My husband has told me quite a different story," she said in a whisper with a grin. "When you took dinner with His Grace the other night, both you and he looked very much disheveled as if you'd both taken in some rather vigorous exercise."

"Oh, I…" Heat filled her cheeks, but there was no judgment or shock in the other woman's face, only polite inquiry. "I don't know where to even begin. Suffice it to say, there might be some scandal between us, but nothing that will damage him or his reputation."

"What about yours?" Mrs. Travers said with a raised eyebrow. "Being with a man in such a delicious way is one thing, but having said relationship with such a high-ranking man carries with it the opportunity for gossip unless you are very careful."

Cate waved away the concern. "I am not a fortune hunter, if that is what you are getting at."

"No, no, of course not." The cook shook her head with a frown. "I didn't mean that at all." She briefly touched Cate's arm. "What I meant was, I am glad the two of you found each other and that there is something between you that warrants such a passionate connection, but…"

"But what?" she asked with a frown. Perhaps in talking with Mrs. Travers, she could sort through her own confusing thoughts.

"But what will you do once your translation duties are finished? Will you continue to see His Grace after that?"

"I don't know, and frankly, it is causing a bit of worry on my part." Again, she looked toward where the duke was hamming it up with his valet and the footmen. A few flutters went through her belly, for he was adorable, and in watching him, no one would ever know that he was a duke, for he treated everyone with the same respect. "He hasn't indicated a need to extend whatever it is we currently share, and I certainly won't ask, for that will make me seem desperate."

"Perhaps, but you have a right to know if he intends to throw you over."

Cate snorted. "There is nothing to throw over; it's not as if he has another woman waiting on the sidelines." Then she frowned, for Barr had made an impression on her in the hectic, whirlwind week they'd spent together. "However, he hasn't mentioned anything after the translation or even beyond Christmas." She shrugged. "It doesn't matter. He is a duke, and he has other priorities. I'm certain he doesn't wish to extend a relationship that is purely physical." Was it, though? Then, to her horror and embarrassment, her eyes filled with tears. "I beg your pardon. I hadn't expected to be so emotional this evening."

"You poor dear." Mrs. Travers patted Cate's arm. "Because you are, I'll wager you that there is more between His Grace and you than heat."

As much as she wanted to fall into her new friend's arms and give into the tears of frustration, hope, and confusion, she removed a lace-edged handkerchief from her reticule and then dabbed the corners of her eyes. "Even if I agreed with you, it doesn't matter. He is who he is, and I am who I am. We both have our places in the world, and that is that."

"What a silly thing to think, Miss Pickwick."

She frowned. "How so?"

"From what I've gleaned about your father, he is a researcher on ancient cultures, yes?" When Cate nodded, Mrs. Travers continued. "And that love of learning has leeched into you. Additionally, you adore books and reading, and I'll wager you've had the opportunity to study fairytales from around the world."

"I'm afraid I don't understand what you're trying to tell me."

"Just this." Mrs. Travers leaned forward and kept her voice lowered while the men hooted and called to each other, for the tide had turned in charades. "Don't give up hope. Everyone in those stories felt as you do at some point in their tales, but doesn't love always win in the end? Perhaps you haven't reached that spot in your own story."

"Oh." A bit of the worry she'd carried seemed to clear. "Thank you for that. It helps, slightly."

"You're welcome, and do remember, dear. Even the best of men are only men at their best. They are sometimes blind until someone points out the obvious to them." She chuckled and her eyes reflected that mirth. "Travers is doing that for His Grace, but you must be patient. He'll realize what it is that he feels eventual-ly."

Considerably cheered, Cate grabbed the other woman's hand. "Thank you for that. It's been the best gift." When she'd done shopping, she'd bought the book a pretty lace fan with tortoise-shell spines. A frippery, of course, but something the frugal woman wouldn't have gotten herself, and wasn't that the point of Christmas remembrances?

Eventually, the game of charades concluded with the team her father was on winning over Barr's. The duke was good-natured about it, and grins were exchanged as freely as champagne. He didn't begrudge anyone from imbibing, which only endeared him to her more.

When he brought her a glass and sat on the sofa where Mrs. Travers had just vacated so she could bring in finger foods and small cakes to the sideboard, Barr gave Cate a flute of champagne.

"Did you have a good chat with my valet's wife?"

"I did. She is a lovely woman." As she took a sip of the bubbly wine, tingling went through her nose and prompted a sneeze. "What I appreciate about not only her, but also all your staff is how loyal they are to you. It's refreshing to know that someone so high on the instep treats the people who work for him well."

Though he shrugged, a hint of ruddy color crept up his neck and into his cheeks. "I am of the opinion that a rising tide raises all ships, so to speak, and life is difficult enough for everyone. Why should I go out of my way to make it miserable as well when we all need each other?"

"You are not like most dukes." Of course, how would she know, since he was the only duke—or titled gentleman—that she had familiarity with.

"Is that a good or a bad thing?" he asked with that specific grin that turned her insides to mush.

"I think you already know; otherwise, you would conduct yourself differently." When he landed his intense gaze on her without apparent regard for the people around them, a wave of heat smacked into her body. So much so that she took refuge in a rather large gulp of champagne, which caused her to sneeze once more. "Pardon me. Clearly, I'm not used to the bubbles."

He leaned close enough to put his lips to the shell of her ear, and whispered, "Would that we were alone, for I'd happily take some of this champagne and pour it all over your gorgeous breasts merely so I could lap it up with my tongue."

Trembles shivered down her spine, and she gasped at his daring. "I think you are in your cups tonight, Scarborough." Heat slapped at her cheeks, for she wouldn't mind that scenario at all.

"I am quite sober." With a wink, he lifted his flute in salute to her.

Good heavens, the man is so potent!

Before she could let her mind skitter to wicked places, her father wandered over to the sofa where she and Barr sat. "Are you enjoying yourself, Papa?"

"I am, indeed, poppet." His grin was positively sparkling, and there was a decided twinkle in his eye. "In fact, I came over to inquire as to whether Scarborough wishes to have dancing this evening. It wouldn't take much effort on all our parts to move the furniture and roll back the rugs."

"Aw, how darling you are," Cate said with another rush of tears into her eyes. "I remember you and Mama enjoyed dancing during Christmastide."

"Your mother especially like it when the candles were lit and the illumination glinted on the decorations." Then his glance fell to the windows where Barr had ordered some of the mistletoe hung before an ornate mirror between them. "I miss her."

Cate sobered. She wiped at her tears. I do, too."

The duke stood. "Then, by all means, let us have dancing. I believe one of the maids can play the pianoforte with passing skill. Afterward, perhaps we'll sing some carols to usher in Christmas." As he swallowed the remainder of his champagne, Barr pushed to his feet. "Travers, Ronald, the rest of you, come assist me in moving the furniture as well as the rugs. Miss Pickwick and her father wish for dancing tonight."

A buzz of excitement went through the assemblage in the room. Everyone sprang into action, for it was obvious they all doted upon the duke and were anxious to please him. In short order, the furniture was rearranged into a circle around the floor. The two Aubusson rugs were rolled and then shoved aside. Somehow, Barr managed to unearth a piano and had it moved into the drawing room by two footmen. One of the maids was encouraged to play whatever tunes came to her mind, and since she'd apparently had no formal training, it was amazing to listen to her raw talent.

The first song she played was a fast-paced tavern piece designed for lively country reels. Everyone in the room entered into the spirit of the tune, and much laughter was had as the reel got underway.

Never had Cate seen her father so happy, and he quickly became the central figure of the festivities with his sparkling eyes and reddened cheeks as he led the line of men in the dance. As for Barr, how could she not watch him? He was certainly an elegant form amidst his staff, and when the reel ended, he swept Mrs. Fitch—the housekeeper—over to the mistletoe, positioned her beneath it, and then bussed her cheek. Everyone cheered and hooted with laughter as a deep blush spread over the poor woman's face.

"Who's next?" the duke called out, and to no one's surprise, two of the maids rushed forward for their own buss upon their cheeks.

Mrs. Travers soon followed, and the giggle that escaped her after the duke kissed her cheek was adorable. However, the valet called Barr out with good natured teasing, which had the company laughing all the more.

Her father called on her to be next, and even when Cate protested with embarrassment, Barr said it was a good idea. He then tugged on her hand until she was placed squarely beneath the kissing bough that someone had decorated with a red velvet ribbon.

"This isn't proper, and you know it," she told the duke in a whispered voice, but he didn't let go of her hand. *Please don't make this into a spectacle.*

"It is Christmas Eve, my dear. There is no such thing as proper during a celebration." Yet he winked and maneuvered her to exactly where he wanted her as his staff and her father looked on.

"Though if you want proper, I can thoroughly claim your lips."

"Oh, good heavens, not here," she said in a barely audible voice.

"Very well, then. More's the pity." With a curled finger beneath her chin, he tilted her head backward, peered into her eyes as if he were searching for a truth—or confirmation—to a question he hadn't asked, then he quickly bussed her cheek like he'd done to every other woman in the room. "Happy Christmas, Cate."

"Happy Christmas, Scarborough."

The onlookers erupted into hoots and clapping, while heat burned through Cate's face.

"Enough of the kissing," her father said in his booming voice. "Let us have a waltz." He gestured with a hand. "Everyone, join in. We'll switch partners so every woman and every man has a chance to dance."

She shook her head. "You are quite something tonight," Cate told her father as she wandered over to his side. "What's gotten into you? Where has my quiet, studious father gone?"

"Oh, it's a holiday, poppet. I'm remembering your mother, so it's making me happy." He held out his hand. "Do me the honor of partnering with me first."

"Of course. Who else would I wish to dance with?" And she slipped her fingers into his palm. It was much like her childhood when her parents would host holiday gatherings and gaiety would fill every inch of the house.

"Well, for one, Ronald the footman has been making eyes at you," her father said with a large grin as he swept her into his arms. "And for another, Scarborough is ready to eat his heart out for not thinking to reserve your time in this dance ahead of me."

"I don't believe that for a second." But a wave of happiness filled her being, and when the maid began to play the melody of a waltz that was popular a few years ago, her father guided her into the first steps while everyone else scrambled to join the makeshift dance floor.

"Then you must be blind, my girl. Unless I miss my guess?" He chuckled as they made the first turn, and he lowered his voice. "The duke is halfway in love with you even if he doesn't know it yet."

"Do stop, Papa. None of that is true." Yet her heartbeat accelerated all the same.

"It would seem that during the course of translating that Egyptian book, you have managed to snag the duke's interest in you for far more than a couple of trysts."

Heat went through her cheeks again. "Hush now. That's gammon."

"I don't know. You are quite an interesting woman."

It was on the tip of her tongue to ask him to stop talking about the duke, but then her father trod on her hem when he encouraged her to twirl. She lost her balance, and with a cry, Cate fell to the floor, but on the way down, the back of her head knocked against the corner of the ornamental screen in front of the cheerful flames in the grate.

Pain screamed through her head, so much so that she swore she saw stars in her eyes before darkness encroached on the edges. As she slumped onto the floor, she was vaguely aware that the activity in the room had come to a sudden halt. Gasps and murmurs echoed in the room, and the sound of quick footsteps rang in her head.

"Cate!" Then Barr was there, kneeling beside her, gently hauling her into his lap. "Good God, there's blood," he said to someone nearby. "We need supplies immediately."

She glanced up into his face, oddly comforted by the fact that he was there. The strength of his arms around her encouraged her to relax into his hold. "It's the curse," she managed to murmur, but when she tried to say more, her lips moved yet not sound came forth.

"Catherine, Cate, stay with me." He gave her a tiny shake. "Fight the urge to sleep. Can you do that for me? Stay with me," the duke repeated, and there was much concern in his tone.

"My head hurts," she whispered, and she wondered why because she could remember what had happened that had sent her to the floor. "The curse..." As cold panic welled, she tried to focus on his face. "Don't... leave... me."

Blackness at the edges of her vision grew overwhelming. It obscured the sight of his pale face, kept coming until she couldn't discern the blue pools of his eyes, and as she tried to raise a hand to touch his face, the creeping darkness engulfed her, dragged her down into a pit with icy fingers.

"Cate!"

No amount of effort on her part could keep her into the present, and with a tiny sigh of surrender, she slipped into that void.

CHAPTER SIXTEEN

December 25, 1816
Christmas morning

T HE LONGCASE CLOCK on the second floor softly chimed the midnight hour. It was officially Christmas morning in London, but Barr felt anything but joy.

In fact, he was nearly worried sick.

After Cate's accident, the party had ground to a halt, and rightfully so. He'd taken charge of the situation while the housekeeper and Mrs. Travers sprang into action to fetch supplies they might possibly need. Barr had carried her upstairs, tucked her into a guest room, then the women had fussed over her while he and Professor Pickwick stood ineffectually by her bedside. However, she hadn't regained consciousness in that bit of time. When he'd put forth the idea that he should summon a doctor, Mrs. Travers said to let her be for a few hours, then she kicked everyone out of the room.

The professor had gone home, but cautioned that if things made a turn for the worse, he needed to be informed immediately. Most of the staff had gone home as well, since the morrow was Christmas and they were given that day of the year off anyway. Travers and the cook stayed behind to help with things should Cate take a turn.

With nothing else to do, Barr retreated to the study to think over everything with his head in his hands and his heart in his throat. Good God, but that had been a singular moment in time where the thought of seeing Cate hurt or possibly killed due to this curse or whatever it might be had acted as a bucket of water thrown into his face.

She'd made quite the impression on him in the past week, and now he admired her more than he probably should. To the point of having his heart involved. Strange but true, and what was more, he didn't mind. Was it too soon? Did it matter? At his age and with his title, should he steer clear of anyone not of the *ton*?

There were no easy or ready answers, yet his mind felt as if it would spin free of his head.

And he remained sitting like that, agonizing over his thoughts, but when the long-case clock chimed the next hour, Travers came into the room.

"Your Grace, you should be abed."

Barr snorted. "How can I retire knowing that Catherine might be fighting for her life? Knowing that she's fallen into this state in my own house during an absurd celebration?"

"None of that." The valet sat in one of the leather chairs that faced Barr's desk. "The impromptu party was everything proper and lovely. What happened to Miss Pickwick was naught but an unfortunate accident. You can't blame yourself."

"Well, I am. If it wasn't for me and finding that damned book, perhaps she would even now..." His words faltered. "I never should have engaged her to work the translation. Then she would have been safe from the fucking curse upon that book." Unshed tears rose in his throat, graveling his voice and urging him to give into that emotion. He shook his head. "Now, because of me, *because* of that curse, she's lying unconscious with an uncertain diagnosis."

Heavy silence met that statement.

Then Travers cleared his throat. "In light of this new development, I feel that I should confess to something."

With a frown, Barr took his head from his hands and stared at his long-time friend. "What do you mean?"

"Uh…" Travers tugged on the knot of his cravat, which was a sure sign that he was bothered by something. "Regarding the curse…"

"Yes?" Barr straightened his spine. "What of it? Spit it out, man." It wasn't like his valet to dicker about.

"I am embarrassed to report that the curse was something my wife and I came up with." His swallow was audible. "We, uh, invented such a thing in an effort to bring you and Miss Pickwick together after I saw how well the two of you got on, especially since you have been so taken with her."

For the space of a few seconds, Barr stared at his friend. "I beg your pardon?" Shock plowed into him as if Travers had physically punched him.

Slowly, Travers nodded. "There is no curse. It is completely made up a bit of fiction to help bring you and Miss Pickwick together as a couple."

"You did this? How?" He couldn't make sense of the admission.

"My wife and I, yes." The valet blew out a breath. "It was simple enough. Mention a curse to you both, and the power of suggestion did the rest. However, we *did* help things along a bit, like loosening the fastenings on the mirror—"

"She could have been seriously injured!"

"—or string a bit of fishing line across the stairs when you were on the move—"

"I could have killed myself in that fall!"

It seemed that Travers wouldn't be interrupted, for he sailed on. "Of course, I couldn't arrange for you to fall out of the tree in Hyde Park, so I… urged Ronald to perhaps jostle you enough during the climb that you might lose your balance."

"Bloody hell, Travers, I could have broken bones."

"But you didn't, and that resulted in Miss Pickwick rushing over in concern, allowing you to kiss her." The valet shrugged. "However, I couldn't have predicted that her father would have stepped on her hem or that she would have fallen and hit her head." He sobered, and there was immense concern in his eyes, heightened by the guttering candlelight. "I am very sorry, Your Grace. We meant no harm, just wanted to see you happy with this woman who has apparently captured your attention."

He supposed he couldn't hold the invention of a curse against his friend, for he meant well, yet Cate was doing poorly, and for that, he just couldn't grant forgiveness. "What the hell am I supposed to do now? She might die."

"She won't."

"What if she doesn't wake?"

"She will."

Barr heaved out a breath. "I need advice."

"Obviously." When the valet chuckled, a slight growl escaped Barr, and his friend once more went serious. "If I may speak freely? Don't be daft, Your Grace. Declare yourself. Ask for her hand."

"What?" Another round of shock slammed into him. "That's a bit mad, don't you think?"

"Then stay here for another few hours and give it a think. Don't you truly believe it's madness, what you feel for Miss Pickwick?"

"I..." He shook his head. "Love? Is that what I'm feeling? Surely not. That wasn't how it went when I was with my wife."

"Gammon." Travers briefly rubbed his fingers over his eyes. "Perhaps you are more of an arse than I thought." With a huff, he narrowed his gaze. "Here's the truth. Any fool can see you're besotted with her."

A grunt escaped him. "Only because we've been copulating like frantic rabbits."

"Clearly." The valet chuckled. "However, it's more than that. I can see it in how you look at her. And the fact that you are so worried? How devastated you were when she was hurt accidentally? There is more there than just heat."

That brought back the unsettled feeling into his chest, where the pressure there sought to steal his breath. Would she come out right? He blew out a breath. "I might not forgive you this, Travers. It was bloody rude of you. And reckless." However, the longer he thought about it, the more it perhaps made sense, for each of those incidents had brought him and Cate closer in ways that sharing carnal pleasures with her never did.

"You will, especially once you secure her hand." The valet offered a slight grin. "That *is* the next logical step, you know."

"Secure her hand?" He stared at his friend. "You want me to ask her to marry me?" The shock broke through his melancholy and guilt from the accident. "Is it possible? So soon after meeting her?" Why did he suddenly feel so scattered?

"Why not?" Travers shrugged. "Life is odd at best. No two women are the same. Neither are any two courtships." One of his blond eyebrows rose in question. "Keep in mind that you are at a different time in your life now. What you needed twenty-five years ago isn't the same as what you need in *this* stage."

That made more sense than it should have. "What if she declines?" That was always a fear of offering one's heart to someone.

"Then she does." His expression suggested it wasn't the end of the world. "But you have enjoyed yourself since making her acquaintance. You've stopped hiding so much, and have even made a friend." When he paused, apparently thinking over his next words, Travers slowly shook his head. "I'll wager you have even learned that life isn't as frightening as you thought since losing your wife. You *can* try again for love and romance, and with the advent of Miss Pickwick, you've been given the perfect opportunity."

"Perhaps, but love? Do you truly believe I'm in *love* with her?" Why was this concept so difficult for him to grasp?

"Only you can answer that, Your Grace, but I have known you for years. I saw how you were with Her Grace, and there was no denying you loved her to distraction." A sigh escaped him. "Yet that romance ended, sadly, when your wife died. That is the natural way of things. You'll always remember her in a portion of your heart, but you have so much capacity for more, and Miss Pickwick has certainly caught your interest, in more ways than one, I'll wager."

"This is… true."

Where he'd previously thought that he might be gutted once her translation services weren't needed because he wouldn't see her daily, those feelings went deeper than that. She brought excitement and new meaning to his days. He looked forward to her arrival each afternoon, for she lifted his spirits and kept him from retreating into himself. But love? Did he have *those* feelings for her? After a week?

Perhaps. What would his life be without her in it? If he were honest with himself, he would admit that he wished to share the remainder of it with her, and in a greater way than just coming together in carnal ways.

He stared at Travers as the sweet confirmation of the decision he didn't realize he'd been struggling to make sent a feeling of peace through his form. Then he nodded. "Perhaps you are correct, Travers. I shall, uh, talk it over with Miss Pickwick the moment she wakes, and perhaps that will happen today. It *is* Christmas, after all. The season of miracles."

"Please relieve your mind. I don't believe her injuries are as severe as you think."

"From your lips to God's ears." Slowly, Barr nodded as his spirits began to lift. "First, I need to go through the jewels in my safe for a certain parure, a certain ring." In fact, the collection he had in mind had sat in that safe for years and years. It wasn't something his wife had favored, and he hadn't wished to gift it to his daughter because it didn't seem fitting. Now he knew why, because it was perfect for Cate.

Waiting all along.

"Good man." The valet nodded as he stood. "I wish you the best and with good tidings. The arrival of Miss Pickwick has been the best thing for you in recent years."

"Perhaps." As much as Barr wanted to say humbug, the fact was he no longer felt that way. "Go home, Travers. Take your wife and go home. Snuggle with her. Hell, fuck her senseless tonight of all nights and be grateful." With a laugh, he gave his friend a wink. "Happy Christmas, my friend."

The valet's grin was a cheeky as his own. "Thank you, Scarborough. Happy Christmas to you as well."

Barr waved him off. "The household has already retired. There is nothing else for you to do at the moment. I don't want to see either you or Mrs. Travers until noon on Boxing Day." When the valet began to offer a protest, he shook his head. "If I require breakfast, I'll get it my damned self."

"Yet Christmas dinner, Your Grace…"

Damn, he'd forgotten those plans. "Right. Well then, you two enjoy yourselves until the evening. Dinner will be a small affair, with just Miss Pickwick—if she's feeling well—and her father in attendance, as well as the two of you. For now, go." Again, he gestured him away.

"Very well." Travers laughed. "Might I insist you go to bed as well?" Then he winked. "Perhaps sharing that bed with a certain ruined librarian might prove the best thing for you during this season."

"Perhaps you're right." And he grinned.

CHAPTER SEVENTEEN

A COUPLE OF hours later, with the linen-covered jewelry coffin containing the parure he'd searched for in hand, Barr paused in front of the door to the guest room where he'd taken Catherine. For the space of a few heartbeats, he stared at the wood panel through the dark as the long-case clock on the second floor chimed the three o'clock hour. Then he raised his free hand and rapped softly on the door.

When that didn't provoke an answer, he pressed the latch and then let himself into the room. Dark and shadows filled the space, but as he approached the bed, he frowned. The linens were rumpled, yet the professor's daughter was not in the bed nor in residence. Dear God, was she wandering the house, confused about where she was due to the bump on the head? Concern tightened his chest as he exited the room and pulled the door closed behind him. Clearly, she hadn't been in the study, and after the Travers went home, he'd gone up to his own suite to dig through his safe.

Where the devil was she?

Thinking to put the parure back into his suite, Barr made his way back to his rooms. Perhaps he should change his clothes in any event, especially if he needed to go out into the night and the snow to search for her, but when he entered his bedchamber, in the soft glow of the candlelight, he spied Cate lounging in the middle of his four-poster bed with the Egyptian book in her hand, reading.

His gasp gave away his intrusion. "Cate. You are awake."

"I am." When she glanced at him, her eyes were clear, and she seemed in possession of all her faculties.

"What are you doing here?" Seeing her in his private space, in his bed, set his imagination soaring. Out of all the rooms in this townhouse they'd coupled in, this suite wasn't one of them. "For that matter, how are you feeling?"

"I am well enough. My head only hurts slightly, and there is a bump at the back, probably from where I fell."

"But, you should be resting—"

"I will. Eventually, but I couldn't calm my mind."

"Why?"

When she gave him a slow, mysterious smile, his world tilted. "I've been waiting for you."

"Why?" He'd been reduced to dull questions, it seemed.

"When I woke, I was in an unfamiliar place, and I was a bit frightened, but then Mrs. Travers came in and talked with me, told me what happened." She set the book aside. "Then she left me a gorgeous night dress and helped me to change into it." When she shrugged, he realized what she was wearing. The night dress in a pale-yellow color edged with lace had once belonged to his wife, but there were no maudlin feelings surrounding that, for clothes were clothes, and it looked entirely different on her than it had on Meredith.

And damn if he wasn't fully aroused.

"That makes sense, I suppose, but why are you in *my* rooms?" He'd purchased her a few presents for the day that had been forgotten in the aftermath of her spill, but one of them was a navy gown with a silver lace overlay, and he couldn't wait to see her in it.

All of that could wait.

"I missed you." Again, she smiled, and he was lost. "I wanted to reassure you that I was all right because I knew you would worry, consider what happen your fault, when it was the curse all along." A chuckle left her throat, and it was the most glorious sound. "Or rather, it wasn't. Mrs. Travers told me she and her husband invented that bit to bring us closer together." This time her smile was blinding in the dim illumination. "Isn't that adorable?"

"That is debatable." The remainder of her his heart that was available for sharing flew into her keeping, and quite honestly, that was the safest place for it. "You missed me?"

That admission lodged in his chest and formed blanketed his heart with warmth.

"Yes, of course."

"Why?" Had this been what he'd been reduced to? A man who couldn't stop gawking at a woman, standing there with his tongue stuck to the roof of his mouth and only talking in one-word responses?

"Because you are *always* uppermost in my mind, and it's Christmas. I wanted to wish you merry and be the first."

Oh, God.

"I appreciate that." Finally encouraging his brain to connect with the remainder of his body, Barr stumbled over to his bureau and put the jewelry coffin on top of it, but while his back was to her, he removed a small ring box from within. "Happy Christmas to you as well."

"Is my father still here?"

"No." After bringing the box over to the bedside table, he left it there then began the task of stripping down to his fine lawn shirt and breeches. For whatever reason, it certainly didn't feel like Christmas. On the other hand, there was a glorious joy that slipped through his person, leaving trails of heat behind. "He was rather ineffectual here, and though he was worried about you, I thought it best to send him home where he was comfortable. If things had taken a turn, I would have sent someone to fetch him."

She nodded. "Understandable, but will you send a missive to

him and let him know I am suffering no ill effects from the spill?"

"Of course. I'll do it at first light." As his nerves felt strung too tight, Barr perched on the side of the bed. He couldn't touch her, not yet, for once he did, there would no going back, and he wouldn't stop until he'd made love to her at least twice. "Are you certain your head is well? Your brain hasn't been damaged? Can you remember your name?"

A snort escaped as she briefly rolled her gaze to the ceiling. "Catherine Anne Pickwick. Spinster at age nine and thirty, daughter of Professor Arthur Pickwick and Mary Pickwick."

"Who am I?"

"The Duke of Scarborough, one of the most handsome men I've ever seen, and collector of rare books." When she frowned, he nearly threw himself on his knees to plead with her until she smiled again. "Outside of your name of Barrington, I'm afraid I don't know your surname; you never told me."

"Combes-Mead."

"How lovely." She folded her hands in her lap atop the counterpane. "You were married to…" Again, she frowned. "You never told me your wife's name."

"Meredith. Her, uh, name was Meredith."

She nodded. "And you lost her five years ago."

"Yes."

"You have two grown children."

"I do."

"And in just the past week you discovered a book of erotic Egyptian prose that you were anxious to have translated, which is how you and I met. And within that week, you fell out of a tree trying to fetch mistletoe, God only knows why."

He cleared his throat. "Because I'm a fool. In some odd part of my mind, I wished to link a tradition of my past with something—or someone—I'd hoped to secure to my future." If he stumbled over his words, she didn't say anything.

"Now *that* I understand." When she looked at him, drew her gaze slowly over his person, he shivered as if she'd physically touched him. "There is nothing wrong with my brain, Barr. Please stop worrying." She raised a hand and explored the back of her head, wincing as she did so. "It's quite tender and there's a knot, but Mrs. Travers said the metal screen barely broke the skin." In the dim light from the candle at the bedside, her pupils were enlarged but not due to the bump on her head. Pure desire was reflected in those brown depths. "Can we please move past my accident and talk about the things that truly matter in this moment?"

"Right." Was she thinking along the same lines as he? Unable to tell, Barr picked up the ring box and pressed it into her hands. "This is for you."

She frowned. "What's this?" As she opened the faded, blue linen box, she sucked in a breath as the candlelight caught on the large oval-shaped amethyst surrounded by tiny round diamonds all set in gold. It was a beautiful piece, and he couldn't wait to see it on her finger.

"A ring." Could she not see that?

"Now whose brain has been shaken?" When she met his gaze, one of her eyebrows raised. "I mean, why are you giving it to me?"

"Oh." Heat rose up the back of his neck. There was no more time to hide. "Uh, I would like you to marry me."

"Marry you." It wasn't a question, but there was shock in her expression as she bounced her gaze between him and the ring. "I'm afraid I don't understand, and if this is out of some sort of misplaced obligation, so help me, Barr, I will walk right out of this townhouse."

"I believe you would, but you would soon freeze, for it's snowing and those clothes will provide little protection." Then he sobered, and feeling far too restless to remain perched on the edge of the bed, he stood to pace the length of the room. "I've already bungled it, haven't I?"

"Truthfully? Yes." She followed his progress with her gaze. "Why do you want me to marry you? And do bear in mind that

I've already told you the one condition on why I would ever say yes to a man."

His spirits tumbled. Did that mean she didn't feel the same about him? There was only one way to find out. "We've known each other for barely a week."

"This is true."

"And while I originally hired you on for translation services, there is something burning between us that can't be denied."

She nodded. "This is also true."

Well, fuck me. What did he need to say? And why is this so much harder than it had been the first time 'round?

Finally, he sighed. "I don't want you in my life merely to relieve carnal urges."

"Meaning what, exactly?" One of her dark eyebrows rose in challenge. "I need to hear your whole declaration, Scarborough, for I refuse to make it easy on you."

"That would be cheating a bit, wouldn't it?" When she nodded, he blew out a breath. "Perhaps it's just as well. I don't want to start this next phase with lack of courage." What to say, though? Did it matter? "Put quite baldly, I've somehow fallen madly into love with you."

Her gasp sounded overly loud in the silent space. "What?"

"I love you." As he nodded, his spirits rose once more. "There are no words, I think, that can adequately describe how it happened or why or even when. All I know is that those feelings weren't there and then they were." He shoved a hand through his hair. "It didn't come on softly like what happened with my wife. Instead, these feelings have plowed straight into me, knocked me tip over tail, and have left me gasping in the aftermath, but that's just it. Perhaps love is different every time."

"Oh, Barr." Cate frowned at the ring resting on the blue faded satin, then glanced at him. "You needn't keep on, for I understand what you're trying to say."

"You do?" Relief slid down his spine.

"Yes." She nodded. "For I feel the same. At first, there was just the heat, but as I spent time with you, watched you, came to know you better, saw how the staff adores you, I've become taken with you, and I'm rather convinced I've been thrust into love with you despite knowing I'm all too wrong for you."

"What the devil does that mean?" Happiness had taken up residence in his chest… until she'd said those last words.

With a shrug, she looked at him. "You're a duke, and I'm nobody."

"Botheration, woman, that matters not to me."

"It might matter later, and to your children, surely."

"I doubt it. They were raised better than that, and at the heart of the matter, they would only wish me happiness. My daughter, especially, has told me that enough times." He rested his hands on his hips. "When all is said and done, though, it is *my* life, and I want you to share it with me."

Emotions warred on her face. "How can you think I'm duchess material?"

"Why do you assume you're not?"

"I'm not of the *ton*."

"And I'm not an archeologist, but that doesn't dim my intentions of sponsoring a dig in Egypt in the next few years."

"Of course you would choose to be stubborn about this," she said with the shake of her head as she plucked the ring from its box. "I mean there will probably be gossip about us."

"Gossipmongers can go hang, but if you truly wish to give them fodder, we could arrange to have intercourse in Hyde Park."

"Don't be indecorous, Barr." The note of scolding in her voice made him grin.

"Ha. Don't pretend you don't enjoy that. I have a feeling if I wasn't at least a bit daring, you wouldn't have lingered around, would you?" Excitement buzzed through his veins, for he was on the downhill side of convincing her.

"Probably not, for I adore a challenge." When she slipped the amethyst ring onto the fourth finger of her left hand, he held his breath. "That is just one of the many reasons why I am accepting your suit, though I might be rubbish as a duchess." As she spoke, Cate left the bed, and when she came to stand before him, he could finally breathe again. "For you, though, I'm willing to try."

The purest joy poured over him as he caught her in his arms. "I'll be with you every step of the way, but first, I must tell you that once the wretched weather is over or there is a bit of a break, you and I are going away on a wedding trip, to anywhere you wish, damn everything else."

Amusement danced in her eyes. "All of that sounds amazing, and I can hardly believe this is happening to me, but above all that? Knowing that I'm quite firmly in love with a man who isn't stuffy or stodgy thrills my heart." She laid a hand on his chest. "Even if you were a pauper, the steadfastness and honor of your person would shine through." With her hair loose and flowing about her shoulders and clad in that night dress, she was every bit the siren of his dreams. "Thank you for being a decent man." Her pink toes peeked out from beneath the hem of her night dress.

"You are welcome, of course, but I thought you wished for an indecent one?" Wanting nothing more than to tumble into bed, he snaked an arm about her waist, but he kept control of those impulses. She would be his soon enough.

"One of the lovely things about you is that you are both." Her grin widened, and his world tilted. "It is merely one of the reasons you've managed to win my heart, I think."

"I don't know what to say." His vow to keep his urges in check fractured when she laid a palm against his chest. The gemstones in the ring he'd given her sparkled in the dim candlelight. In a few moments, he would have her in his bed, and if he were fortunate, they wouldn't leave until it was time for Christmas dinner.

"Why say anything, then?" A giggle escaped her, and he would die a thousand deaths to hear that sound again. Her fingers slipped over the fabric of his fine lawn shirt, and the heat of her seeped into his skin. "Will there be much more talking, do you think? There are other, more urgent, endeavors I'd like to get to."

"Somehow, I don't think I'll be able to survive a life with you." He could scarcely breathe from the sudden overwhelming emotions that crowded into his throat. "Imagine, me married a second time. I didn't think it was possible."

She laid a palm against his cheek. "Everything is once you start living."

"Or stop hiding beneath research and in the stacks at the lending library?"

Another laugh came from her, and the feeling of falling assailed him. "Yes, exactly. Perhaps we are well matched after all. At least we have the love of books between us."

"And to think forbidden words have bound us…" Barr laid his hand over hers, turned his head, and then pressed a kiss into her palm. Then, because he couldn't stand it any longer, he tugged her into his arms. "Damn, but you feel good."

"So do you, but I honestly think we both have far too many clothes on," she whispered. Then, holding his head between her hands, Cate pulled back enough to peer into his eyes. "Thank you for choosing me."

"How could I not? You are arresting and enchanting, and you sometimes smell like books, and I adore your mind." He rested his forehead on hers. "This happiness, this looking forward to marriage a second time around, frightens me."

"You wouldn't be human if it didn't. I'm scared too about a few things, but we will meet all the challenges together." She rose onto her toes and pressed her lips to his. "And I suspect you'll have fun this time around without needing to worry about producing an heir or attending to your title."

"True." Excitement buzzed at the base of his spine. "Perhaps after the new year I will write to my mother and children, as well as my sister, and tell them the news. Hopefully, by Easter, we can manage to gather together so everyone can meet you."

"I hope they like me." Such love glimmered in her eyes, another round of emotions beset him.

"How can they not? *I* adore you after only a week." Then, because he couldn't stand it another moment longer, Barr settled her into his arms and kissed her, drank from her, showed her without words how much she was coming to mean to him. Tangling his hands into her long tresses, he urged her head backward and deepened the embrace.

Silk slid along satin as their tongues danced and dueled. Tiny fires erupted through his blood and that heat fueled his hunger for her. Easily, he worked at the ties of her satin and lace robe and urged it from her shoulders. The nearly sheer material fell with a whisper to the floor. She plucked at his shirt. A low growl escaped him, for he was obliged to break the kiss to shed the garment only to toss it to the floor. Then her fingers glanced over his chest and abdomen, dancing, stroking, caressing, and he thought he might die from the heaven of that touch.

"Cate…" Both needing to feel her everywhere on his person and not wanting her to extend the torture, he sucked in a breath. "I want you naked and in my bed. We've not coupled there yet."

"I haven't bid you nay, Scarborough." The way those smoky tones uttered his title had his shaft hardening faster than if she'd teased it. While she held his gaze, Cate slowly, so damn slowly, removed the thin night dress. When it pooled on the floor at her adorable feet, a breath shuddered from him. "If you don't put us both on the bed post haste, I swear I will start without you."

Oh, dear God. As much as he celebrated her boldness when it came to carnal matters, she might indeed be the death of him. "Like hell you will, Miss Pickwick." The breeches proved problematic when he got a foot stuck in one of the legs. She watched him with a mix of amusement and desire in her expression that didn't help as she crawled into the bed, but finally he had the foot free. Seconds later, he joined her beneath the bedclothes and covered her body with his.

The warmth of her called to him; the faint floral scent of her teased his senses, hurtled him further into arousal.

"Finally nude, and every bit as wonderful as I thought." Her whisper in the room with the snow leaving lacey shadows on the window and walls enhanced the intimacy of the moment. "I can't wait to explore all of you." She peppered the underside of his jaw with kisses, nipped a line along the column of his throat.

"We have the whole night, and the house is ours. Only two maids live in." While he made love to her mouth, he teased a breast with his hand. A moan sounded from the back of her throat and her spine arched, for she enjoyed it when he flicked and rolled her nipples.

"Good, because I might need you more than once this Christmas morning." Cate urged a hand between their bodies. When she cupped his shaft and stones, he sucked in a breath, for he was so hard that he might pop off at any moment. "Will I ever stop marveling about this part of you?"

"God, I hope not." Her touch was both heaven and hell, but he didn't bid her nay. Pleasure pulsed through his veins, concentrating in his length. With every stroke, with each brush of her fingers, he hurled closer to the edge of bliss.

Needing a distraction, Barr delved a hand between her splayed thighs. Easily he encouraged the swollen nubbin at her center out of hiding, and seconds later after strumming his finger over it, circling it, alternating degrees of friction, she uttered a strangled sort of scream as she fell into a gentle release.

"You must have been in great need since you fell into that so quickly." It was but one of the things he loved about her.

"It's the company I've been keeping." She squeezed his stones and chuckled at his moan. Just as he thought to play at her nubbin again, her fingers glanced over the highly sensitive skin that rested between his stones and anus. The giggle she made when he nearly launched off the bed echoed in his ears, and he welcomed the sound, for it heralded endless moments of happiness and joy—something that had been absent in his life for far too long. "Finish me, Barr. I cannot wait for extended foreplay tonight."

"As if I could deny you anything." He rested the bulk of his weight on his forearms while aligning his tip at her opening.

"I can't believe we are to marry." She looped her arms about his shoulders, wriggled into a better position, and bumped her hips against his, while offering a grin. "Beyond that, I need to feel you inside of me."

Bloody hell but he was so damned fortunate he could hardly bear it. There was no more time to set aside for thinking. Desire and need took command. With a powerful flex of his hips, he penetrated her body, went as deep as he could. Their moans of enjoyment blended together. Every time he was with her in this way was amazing, and he still couldn't believe he'd won her.

Of course, it had only been a week, so it wasn't as if there was such a long period of convincing her.

The bite of her fingernails digging into his biceps competed with the bite of her teeth when she nipped at his earlobe. He gripped her hip with a hand and encouraged one of her legs upward with the other which allowed him to stroke ever deeper into her honeyed heat.

Over and over again, Barr thrust, and she matched his rhythm until they moved effortlessly together in a dance as old as time. The second he peered into the dark pools of her eyes, saw the same emotions reflected there that were flitting through him, he was lost, and he hoped he would never grow bored with this sort of connection.

Eventually, he passed the point of no return. Urgency roared through his shaft and tingled through his stones. Every tiny little sound of encouragement pushed him closer to shattering, and when she slipped a hand down his back to squeeze one of his arse cheeks, he was gone. "Cate!" The hoarse shout sounded overly loud, but he didn't care.

"Oh, yes, Barr, yes. Go harder. Faster."

How could he deny the request? With the last of his strength, he stroked into her with short, deep, fast thrusts until he thought he might completely expire from either the effort or the pleasure beginning to flood his person.

Finally, her body stiffened. A keening cry left her throat. Cate arched her back, gripped his arms so tightly he feared she'd leave bruises, and her thighs quivered. Over and over, she repeated his name. The words pushed through his blood, and then with one powerful stroke, he went tip over tail into the void of bliss where nothing existed except extreme, soul-breaking sensation that made him feel both comforted, satisfied, and as if he'd died at the same time.

All because of this one woman.

"Damnation," he whispered against the side of her neck as he came back to himself. Sweat dampened his back while he struggled to regulate his breathing.

She chuckled, but the sound was a bit on the tired side. "I heartily enjoyed that." As she drew a hand along his chest, the tickle of her fingers through the sparse hair there nearly sent him to heaven once more if that was even possible. "It seems my choice of husbands will certainly keep me happy."

"I am glad you're so satisfied." When she nodded, he flashed her a tired grin. "You're certain you wish to be my duchess?"

"Yes. The new challenge will give me a voice to help fight illiteracy in London and perhaps make books not quite so expensive."

"If anyone can do it, you can." Barr resettled on the bed next to her on his side. "I love you. We will have an interesting marriage, I'll wager."

"Punctuated by books, research, poking through ancient places, and carnal explorations." She bussed his cheek and then burrowed into him while wrapping an arm about his waist. "I can't wait."

"Neither can I." He wrapped his arms around her and simply held her in the silence. Everything in his life had changed, or would soon, because of her. Travers would certainly make jest of him, but he didn't care. "What need have we for an erotic manual when there are intuition and soft emotions between us already?" Then he frowned. "Do you think it's too soon or that we are misguided?"

"Not at all. There is no timeline or rules for how love behaves between two people." When the candle finally guttered out and the acrid scent of smoke filled the air, she sighed. "By the by, I finished the translation."

"What?" Shock smacked into him. "When?"

"A few hours ago. I was bored after waking, so once Mrs. Travers and I spoke, she brought me the book and my notes."

He frowned. "Was it by her urging that you accepted my offer of marriage?"

"No, but I took her advice under consideration. It was adorable how she and your valet wished us matched, but ultimately, the choice was mine." She brushed her lips over his. "You have my heart, Barr. That is all."

That mollified him. "Tell me how the book ends."

"Very well." After struggling onto her back, she rested her head on his shoulder while his arms came about her. "The pharaoh's son successfully sent his lover away to safety. He arranged for a boat to carry her down the Nile to a port he considered safe, where a family loyal to him had agreed to take her in."

He gasped. "He didn't go with her?" How could any man send the woman he loved away without accompanying her?

"Apparently not. Things at the palace grew more urgent. Instead, while his love went to safety, the man searched out the person who'd betrayed them both. From what I could tell, the pharaoh's son challenged him to a fight."

That made sense. If someone betrayed Cate and affected her safety, he would go after them. "Did he win?"

"Unfortunately, I don't think so, but the book was badly damaged in that section and much of the text is missing, so it's only conjecture on my part."

"How disappointing." Barr frowned. "Is that all?"

"More or less." Cate shrugged. "The last line on the last page says basically says, 'Keeper of my heart, I will live on in that organ as well as in the life within you'."

"What?" Another gasp escaped him. "His lover was pregnant?"

"So it seems."

"No wonder he was frantic to send her away."

She nodded. "I like to think they were reunited somehow, and that they both kept travelling until they were far enough from his father that they could live life as a family in secret. I also like to believe they built a bond of love so strong nothing could break it."

For long moments, he stared at the ceiling that was shrouded in shadows. "I adore how your mind works. I will take comfort in your ending."

"Oh, Barr." Taking one of his hands, she threaded their fingers together. "History is sometimes unfair and fraught with horrors and sorrows. In this way, I can perhaps change the narrative to instill hope for the future in whomever happens to read the book next."

"But no one will know of the real ending."

"Perhaps it's not *for* everyone to know. A reader can make of it what they will once you sell the book."

"No." He shook his head. "I have decided to keep the book."

"Why?" Yet curiosity propelled that one-word inquiry into the air.

The heat of embarrassment went through his chest. "It is how we met, and it is part of *our* story now. The book will remain in my library—our library—and it will be part of how we'll tell people that we are engaged." Pausing to press a kiss into the top of her head, he then said, "But for now, it's our secret, the story of our own forbidden words, and our memories of this time will be ours alone."

A soft sigh left her throat. "You're a sweet romantic."

"Well, I just know what I like." He held her closer. "Happy Christmas, Catherine."

"Happy Christmas, Barrington."

He grinned. "Damn, I can't wait to announce our news, but

for now, I'm content in keeping it to ourselves." After all, he'd won her, had her finally in his bed, and intended to claim her body many more times between now and the new year. Everything else could wait.

To think that one tiny, almost insignificant story of a pair of lovers from thousands of years ago could have inspired his own second love had the power to stagger his mind. But then, as the book had said, love was love.

Perhaps that was all anyone needed to know. There was a certain comfort in that.

EPILOGUE

December 25, 1819
Christmas Day
Scarborough Expedition House
Giza, Egypt

BARR SENT A glance about the courtyard of his expedition house that lay framed on three sides by the one story building. In the distance, the triangle tops of the Great Pyramids of Giza were visible. He couldn't help but grin, for three years ago, being in Egypt and sponsoring an archeological dig was only a dream. Standing there under the stars, clad in boots, breeches, and a fine lawn shirt rolled up to the elbows and opened at the placket with a gentle breeze ruffling through his hair was, to him, the epitome of success in his life.

This was the second winter season that he and his wife, Cate, had spent in Egypt, and in two months, they would celebrate their second wedding anniversary. They would head back to England in early April, but for now, that seemed like an eternity away.

In the two years since that memorable Christmas, they had made no effort in preventing pregnancy during their frequent couplings, and though there had been a hint of increasing a couple of times, nothing substantial had developed. However, neither of them had been disappointed, for his son had a child now, and his daughter was currently in the early stages of her own pregnancy after marrying six months earlier. There was no end of activity, joy, and laughter at the London townhouse when everyone was in Town, and Barr wouldn't have it any other way.

"You look quite pleased with yourself," Cate said, her voice a purr, as she walked over the stones of the courtyard to his location. The hem of her cotton dress whispered in the relative silence, and the navy color made her blend in with the night around her. "Can I assume there was a significant find today?"

He slipped an arm about her waist, for there wasn't a day that went by when he wasn't so damned grateful for her. Since the day he'd wed her, they had rarely been out of each other's company for more than several hours at a time. "Not large or significant according to Belzoni's standards, of course, but every shard of pottery, every scrap of papyrus with written words are clues to other things. It's all steps in the right direction and the chance to preserve the past."

During their first year in Egypt, he and Cate had agreed to sponsor a portion of Giovanni Battista Belzoni's recent dig. Belzoni was Italian explorer and archaeologist who made significant discoveries including the tomb of Seti I, which is sometimes referred to as Belzoni's Tomb. Since the man was incredibly active in unearthing treasures of Egypt, he'd also cleared the entrance to the great temple at Abu Simbel where he removed a seven-ton bust of Ramesses II, which he sent to England, funded by Barr's generous monetary donation.

However, for the Christmastide season this year, Barr retreated to Giza where he had the expedition house, for since Belzoni had been the first to enter the Pyramid of Khafre, which was the second pyramid of the Giza complex, Barr had decided he would take his team and continue to explore that pyramid in the hopes of finding a new entrance or other treasures. Belzoni didn't mind, for his interests were many and varied throughout the country, and Barr suspected he merely wanted the headlines in the papers more than unearthing the past and preserving it for the future. Besides, he'd been given permission to dig from Belzoni as well as the authorities in Egypt, so he was quite happy with his decision.

Of course, because of Belzoni, knowledge regarding Ancient Egypt in general, and languages and life therein in particular, exploded. He had written a book and had set up a foundation which worked with others to preserve pieces of the past. One of those efforts was to try and prevent the theft and acquisition of great statues and tomb reliefs from being snapped up by wealthy men around the world to grace drawing rooms and such. Shipping mummies back to London was a particularly gruesome hobby for some.

It was that foundation where Cate had found her passion, and she worked closely with it to further her own knowledge regarding the Egyptian world. Barr was convinced that soon, she would make some sort of discovery of her own, on inscriptions or in translations, and he couldn't be prouder of her.

And this year was especially poignant, for his son, Geoffry, had decided to join the expedition, along with his wife, Alice. They had a one-year-old son back in England, being watched over by Alice's parents, and the two young parents had been desperate to get away from parenting duties for a few months. Additionally, the younger couple was celebrating a fourth anniversary, and Barr suspected they had hopes of falling pregnant again.

"Well, regardless of whether or not your team finds anything, this has still been a lovely respite from the dreary weather in London." She turned so that she was securely held in his arms and laid a hand against his cheek. "Congratulations for meeting a long-held dream."

"One of many that have been reached ever since you can into my life."

"Pish posh, Scarborough." But there was pleasure in her smile. "We met. Then opportunities happened. I had nothing to do with it."

"Let us agree to disagree." He grinned and held her gaze with his. "I hope you are hungry for Christmas dinner. Travers tells me that his wife has outdone herself this year." When he'd removed to Egypt, most of his London staff had traveled with him, and that also made him happy, for they were very much his family. Even now, the clink of silverware and crystal drifted to his ears in the courtyard, for the dining room was open with curtains on two sides, just across the courtyard from where they stood.

"I am, actually, and I'm also hoping that you will provide dessert a bit later." The whispered words were full of innuendo that shivered down his spine to burrow through his shaft. "I quite fancy a mad romp in our bedroom."

Oh, God.

He slipped his hands to her hips and roughly drew her against him. "I think we can arrange that. After all, it *is* Christmas." Then, because he could, and he was a damned duke, he claimed her lips in an intense kiss that saw them both breathless in short order. That was how it always was between them. The passion between them hadn't faded since they'd met, which had delighted them, and just proved to him that they were indeed well suited.

When Cate pulled away, her grin was on the wobbly side. A shaky sigh escaped her. "That potency certainly hasn't faded since that first Christmas."

Before he could respond, Travers came out to join them in the courtyard. "Rein yourself in, Your Grace," the valet joked. "Dinner is nearly on."

Barr couldn't help but laugh. "Can I help it if I still desperately love my wife?"

"I love mine too, but I can stand to be separated from her for a few hours."

Cate laughed, and the sound of it sent warmth through his chest. "Do behave, Travers. Scarborough is a lovely man." She sent the valet a wink. "Where are you off to?"

He hefted up wooden bucket. "To the well. Need some water for washing the dishes."

Once Travers left, Barr took hold of Cate's hand. "I'll wager there's about an hour until dinner. We can probably slip away for a bit of a pre-dinner nibble."

"I like the way you think, Scarborough. Besides, we *do* need to dress for the meal, and you know how you enjoy helping me with that."

"Absolutely…" And he grinned all the way into the house, along the corridor, and into their shared suite.

Life had only grown better as the years rolled on, and he was so glad he'd accidentally uncovered a book of erotic prose that had led to one of the best things in his life.

Odd how things like that happened.

The End

About the Author

Sandra Sookoo is a *USA Today* bestselling author who firmly believes every person deserves acceptance and a happy ending. Most days you can find her creating scandal and mischief in the Regency-era, serendipity and happenstance in Victorian America or snarky, sweet humor in the contemporary world. Most recently she's moved into infusing her books with mystery and intrigue. Reading is a lot like eating fine chocolates—you can't just have one. Good thing books don't have calories!

When she's not wearing out computer keyboards, Sandra spends time with her real-life Prince Charming in central Indiana where she's been known to goof off and make moments count because the key to life is laughter. A Disney fan since the age of ten, when her soul gets bogged down and her imagination flags, a trip to Walt Disney World is in order. Nothing fuels her dreams more than the land of eternal happy endings, hope and love stories.